Sorceries Zothique

Ran Cartwright

Frogtown Press
2018

Dedicated to

Clark Ashton Smith

whose *Last Continent* inspired these tales

and to

Steve Lines and John B Ford

who gave these tales a home

Publishing History

"Maraeva" in *Lost Worlds of Space and Time, Volume Two* (Rainfall Books, 2005); in *Tales of the Last Continent* (Revolving Nuclear Zoo Machine Productions, 2013)

"Lest Darkness Se Strength" in *Strange Sorcery #4* (Rainfall Books, July 2007); in *Tales of the Last Continent* (Revolving Nuclear Zoo Machine Productions, 2013)

"Glardun's Jewel" in *Tales of the Last Continent* (Revolving Nuclear Zoo Machine Productions, 2013)

"The Snow Crystal" in *Tales of Zothique: In the Latter Days Vol 1,* chapbook (Rainfall Books, December 2007); in *Tales of the Last Continent* (Revolving Nuclear Zoo Machine Productions, 2013)

"A Moment out of Time" in *Tales of Zothique: In the Latter Days Vol 1,* chapbook (Rainfall Books, December 2007); in *Tales of the Last Continent* (Revolving Nuclear Zoo Machine Productions, 2013)

"The Dying Shall Die" in *Tales of Zothique: In the Latter Days Vol 1,* chapbook (Rainfall Books, December 2007); in *Tales of the Last Continent* (Revolving Nuclear Zoo Machine Productions, 2013)

"The House of Tuluroch" in *Tales of Zothique: The Final Swan Song Vol 2*, chapbook (Rainfall Books, January 2008); in *Tales of the Last Continent* (Revolving Nuclear Zoo Machine Productions, 2013)

"Night Shades of Ilcar" in *Tales of Zothique: The Final Swan Song Vol 2,* chapbook (Rainfall Books, January 2008); in *Tales of the Last Continent* (Revolving Nuclear Zoo Machine Productions, 2013)

"The Final Swan Song" in *Tales of Zothique: The Final Swan Song Vol 2,* chapbook (Rainfall Books, January 2008); in *Tales of the Last Continent* (Revolving Nuclear Zoo Machine Productions, 2013)

Sorceries Zothique

I am the author and architect of The Book.
I am the author and architect of the world.

from *The Book of Destiny*

Contents

Maraeva

1
The Shadows of Maraeva

The torch light was faint with the street softly aglow. Evil necromancy was in the air, strong and prevalent. Most of Maraeva's residents avoided the streets of the Shunned Quarter at night. Many times citizens had disappeared from dark alleys never to be seen again. Stories ran rampant, strange tales told of how decadent rituals were held behind closed doors, how innocent people died horribly, their souls howling in eternal damnation.

Dark forms lurked at every corner. Cloaked figures slunk in alleys, peering around, only to disappear into a side door of some decaying hamlet to work their strange and terrible magic. Yet, there were those who came to the Shunned Quarter at night, lawless men and wanton women flocking to Maraeva's Shunned Quarter to ply their trade. Those who sought adventure in the lawless dark would come as would the curious who came to witness what was rumored, their foolish curiosity many times bringing about their death.

It was this same curiosity that brought Quen and Taum to the Shunned Quarter of Maraeva. Quen and Taum stood in the shadows of an alley as a cloaked figure silently passed them by. The figure stopped, turned, peered directly into the shadows where Quen and Taum stood concealed. A cold lifeless chill ran down Quen's back. He turned his eyes to Taum. Taum glanced at Quen, shrugging his shoulders. Quen turned, peering out of the shadows at the mysterious figure. The figure was gone. Quen breathed a sigh of relief.

"I don't think we should've come here," Quen said.

"Aye, I agree," Taum replied. "Let's go home."

"Aye," Quen said.

The pair stepped from the shadows into the light of a nearby torch. They peered up and down the narrow alley. From nearby came the agonizing scream of a woman. Down the alley a hunched shadow skulked through an intersection. Quen tapped Taum on the shoulder. The two of them headed down the alley on their way out of the Shunned Quarter.

They confined themselves to the shadows, passing silently along the fronts of small squat wooden buildings that lined the narrow earthen alley. Ahead was another torch mounted in a wall bracket, just beyond another intersection. As Taum and Quen approached the intersection, a cloaked figure suddenly appeared from around the corner. Quen and Taum stopped. There was no doubt. It was the same figure they had seen only minutes earlier.

Slowly, deliberately, the figure approached the two young men. In the light of the torch Quen and Taum saw the lined face of an old sorcerer recessed within the folds of the hood of his cloak. The old sorcerer's hair was white as snow, a white beard disappearing into the folds of the cloak he wore. The furrowed lines of his face were highlighted by the torch light. A grin crept across his face as he stopped before Quen and Taum.

"You come from elsewhere in Maraeva," the old voice creaked, his eyes glittering.

"Ay...aye," Quen stammered, his voice and mind uncertain.

"I can tell by your clothes," the old sorcerer said. "You come to see the Shunned Quarter. You come to see if the rumors are true."

"Aye," Taum said, barely a whisper.

"We were going home...," Quen began.

"Going home?" the old sorcerer creaked. "The night is early. You came here to learn. Do you not wish to learn? There are things here to make your skin crawl!" The old sorcerer paused, his eyes smiling, then he added, "I can show you many things, many wonders, things others have only guessed. You wish to know of these things?"

There was triumph in the old quavering voice, a triumph that was beginning to sway Quen and Taum. Their imagination was stirred.

They had no doubt this sorcerer could show them much. But an inbred fear, a nagging doubt, still clung by a thread.

"Aye, but...," Quen began.

"I can see that you do," the old sorcerer interrupted.

The stare of the old sorcerer frightened Quen momentarily, but curiosity began to rise within him again. There was something in the tone of the old sorcerer's voice - a meaning, a hint, something the old sorcerer knew that Quen, and no doubt everyone else in Maraeva, didn't know. Quen wanted to know.

"All right, show us these wonders," Quen said.

"Quen, should we?" Taum was uncertain.

Quen glanced at Taum, noting the fear and apprehension in Taum's eyes. There was something about the old sorcerer that Taum didn't like. Although Taum wasn't sure why, he was certain their chance association with the old sorcerer would come of ill ends.

"Aye, it's why we're here," Quen replied. "Anyway, I want to know more of the dark secrets of Maraeva. The mysteries. The..."

"Aye, aye, I can see that you do," the old sorcerer interrupted, his voice gleeful. "Let us not waste the hours away. Come. Follow me!"

The old sorcerer turned into the alley he had appeared from. Quen and Taum followed. They hastened down the alley to a small thatched hamlet. A soft orange glow issued from the front windows. Opening the door the old sorcerer led Taum and Quen inside.

The orange glow was the light of a small fireplace. The flames licked at a massive stone mantel. Crackling little swirls of smoke curled into the air. Quen and Taum stood just inside the door as the old sorcerer pulled the hood of his cloak around his shoulders, releasing the long white shock of hair. Pulling his beard from the folds of his cloak, the old sorcerer turned to face Quen and Taum.

"Welcome to my humble abode," he smiled.

The young men peered about the room. It was typical of what they had heard of the abode's of Maraevan sorcerers. The fireplace was carved of stone with strange designs and symbols. A pair of grinning skulls was carved into the fireplace just below the great mantel. The eyes of each skull, made of red gemstones, sparkled in the firelight. On the mantel were two used black candles. In one corner of the room stood an old wooden clock, the brass pendulum long since stopped and choked with a network of cobwebs. Along one wall was an old bookcase containing many old leather bound volumes with titles in languages neither Quen nor Taum could understand. A series of shelves were lined with glass jars containing all manner of sorcerous accouterments. A table in the center of the room and an odd assortment of dusty and worn furniture cluttered the room, some of which gave the appearance of being made for other than mortal man.

"Well, do not dally," said the old sorcerer, gesturing with a hand. "Quickly. Come. You wish to learn."

Quen and Taum slowly approached the table. On the table was a bowl containing a murky red liquid and another black candle. The old sorcerer glanced at the candle, and a flame suddenly danced from the wick. Wide-eyed with disbelief, Taum glanced at Quen, then at the old sorcerer.

"A clever parlor trick," the old sorcerer said. "Any child can do it with practice. But tricks are not why you have come. You want to know the dark mysteries and secrets of Maraeva's Shunned Quarter."

"Aye, I guess so," Quen replied hesitantly.

"The streets are not for everyone," the old sorcerer said, a grin crawling across his furrowed face. "Know that there are many dark secrets in Maraeva, many secrets that I do not even know. There are many that I wish NOT to know. All secrets of the Shunned Quarter stem from the same source. Look into this bowl and you shall see."

The old sorcerer stepped to the edge of the table. He passed a hand over the bowl. The murky red liquid began to clear. Images appeared in the center of the liquid. Dark shadowy things began to form, things remotely resembling wretched men and women. As the dark shapes disappeared, the image of a small village appeared. An ancient blood red sun poured its light upon people scurrying about on their daily errands. There were horse drawn carts going to and from markets. There were children playing in dusty alleys, nearby fields, and what appeared to the main street. People were planting crops and tending gardens. The village was peaceful.

"Maraeva as it was in the beginning many centuries ago," the old sorcerer said.

"What does that have to do with the mysteries?" Taum asked.

"Nothing directly, my boy," the old sorcerer replied. "But the darkness which descended upon Maraeva comes from the village founder, a man who dabbled in the black arts."

"That still doesn't answer my question," Taum said softly.

"Perhaps not," the old sorcerer said. "As you can see, the village of Maraeva was once bright and gay. Then the Founder brought darkness to Maraeva. From that darkness rose the Shunned Quarter."

The old sorcerer passed his hand over the bowl again. The scene changed. Again the village was pictured, but closer. The scene was of the Shunned Quarter. Darkness was upon the streets. There were cries of destitute and agony. Malicious laughter, evil triumph. Death was everywhere, a great pestilence. Carts loaded with bodies were being led from the village. Men and women could be seen crying in anguish along the streets. There were painful rituals and ceremonial deeds degrading to the villagers; bloodletting and sacrifice. In the center of the street walked a tall dark figure clothed in a black hooded cloak. The hood was drawn up, concealing the face.

"The Founder," the old sorcerer said softly. "What you have seen in the rituals still occurs to this day."

"You say that man was the Founder," Quen said, pointing to the image of the mysterious figure in the bowl. "Who was he?"

"That I cannot say," the old sorcerer replied. "Some say he came from Zul-Bha-Sair; others say Cyntrom. It does not matter where he came from or why he came to Cincor. What matters is it was he who brought the shadows of death and the terrible mysteries to this city, the city he himself founded. There is a legend that only he can take the shadows away."

"Take the shadows away?" Taum asked. "How?"

The old sorcerer shot a cold glance at Taum, an eyebrow arched above the sorcerer's left eye. The cold stare melted to an expression of bewilderment. "I do not know. But there is one who does, one who can tell you," the old sorcerer said after a pause. He grinned as he passed a hand over the bowl once again. The red liquid returned to its original murky state as the old sorcerer turned his attention back to Quen and Taum. The two young men remained silent, but the old sorcerer could read questions on their faces.

"You wish to know?" the old sorcerer said. "Well, I will tell you. The old Wizard of Maraeva knows! He can tell you! He can tell you the Founder's name!"

"The crazy old man that lives in the mountain cave outside of town?" Quen asked.

"Aye," the old sorcerer replied. "He knows all."

"I don't think we should go to the mountain," Taum said. "The stories. Everyone stays away from there."

"I don't know," Quen said, staring at the murky red liquid. He glanced at Taum. "Come on, Taum. We should be getting home."

Quen looked at the old sorcerer, smiled, then turned to the door of the hamlet. Taum followed. Quen stopped at the door and turned to face the old sorcerer. He wanted to say something, but found himself mute as he gazed into the deep pools of the old sorcerer's eyes. The old sorcerer, still standing by the table smiled and nodded.

"Seek the Wizard of Maraeva," the old sorcerer said. "He will tell you many things. But when you go to the mountain, beware Geerla of the Mist, the guardian of the wizard's domain!"

Quen and Taum disappeared into the night. The old sorcerer stared at the door, then turned his attention back to the bowl. He passed a hand over it. Another image began to form. It was the image of the Founder of Maraeva. Still the Founder was clothed in the black hooded cloak, his face concealed in the hood. In the image the figure walked slowly down the street. The old sorcerer smiled.

"I wonder if what the old wizard says is true," the old sorcerer voiced his thoughts softly.

2
The Monster from the Mist

The morning sun shown a gloomy red on the desolate landscape of northeastern Cincor. Colored ashen, the surrounding land was nearly barren. Sparse vegetation sprung up among clusters of boulders and rock. The botanical death of a few gnarled old trees dotted the landscape. The air was hot and humid, no breeze for comfort.

To the south the land was mostly level. A narrow ravine ran northeast to southwest, skirting Maraeva by three miles. The ravine, a dry river bed, was strewn with rocks and boulders of varying size. The rocks and boulders clustered as the walls of the ravine rose vertical further to the north, forming a deep gorge. The gorge cut into a narrow band of hills which bred into the Myskrasian Mountains, barely visible on the Maraevan skyline. Tabled into the foothills was a narrow plateau. On the right the plateau dropped a thousand feet into the rocky gorge. On the left, and straight ahead, the plateau merged with the foothills leading to the Myskrasian Mountains.

Quen drew up on the reins of his camel, pulling to a stop atop the plateau. Naura, riding behind him, softened her grip on his waist. Taum, tandem with Isla on another camel, pulled alongside Quen and Naura. Quen glanced at the opposite wall of the gorge, his hands tight on the reins. He had heard the numerous stories of sudden unexplained winds blowing across the plateau near the gorge, sending people, their mounts, and pack animals crashing into the depths. Quen had never seen it happen on the plateau, but the sudden winds were a fact of life in Maraeva. At one time, in Quen's youth, a sudden wind storm had erupted with no warning, sending a thick wall of dust and sand cascading into the streets of the village. When the wind storm subsided the streets of Maraeva were covered in sand several inches deep. The cleanup had taken weeks. Some whispered necromancy as the cause.

"You think we should get off this plateau?" Taum questioned.

"Aye, those wind storms that come from nowhere could kill us," Naura added nervously.

Quen glanced over his shoulder at Naura. He remained silent, his mind still trying to find a reasonable explanation for bringing her and Isla. Naura had insisted. Quen had never learned to say *no* to her. He shook his head, accepting the fact that Naura had insisted on coming along. When the Bonding Ceremony took place between them, Quen would never be able to say *no* to her again.

Secretly Quen wished he had never agreed to the ceremony. His mind wandered, reflecting on a history when there was no such thing as a Bonding Ceremony. *To think, belonging to only one woman! Ridiculous! Unheard of in the Old Times!* Quen shrugged at the thought of his upcoming ceremony and sighed. He knew the ceremony had caused many men to become wretched, running to the

Shunned Quarter to escape, and more often than not, finding only horrible death.

"Aye, we shouldn't be very far from Crown Peak," Quen replied to Taum's question, pushing the Bonding Ceremony from his mind.

Quen shook the reins and the camel plodded toward the gently rolling foothills at the base of the towering mountains, Taum and Isla following close behind. The mountains seemed to rise out of the ground like a wall; the division between foothills and mountains was in marked contrast, the rolling hills giving way abruptly.

Traversing the mountains had become a finely honed art over the years. The dry conditions in the area made the mountainside treacherous, loosely lying gravel and rocks easily dislodged, starting a chain reaction that ended in massive landslides. Many a time had Maraevans been buried alive due to a misplaced footfall of their mounts. Only two weeks previously a couple, only days before their Bonding Ceremony, had been killed in such a manner.

Following a narrow path strewn with clusters of boulders and rocks, they rounded the mountainside that formed the first layer of the Myskrasian range mountain wall. Quen suddenly drew his camel to a stop as they emerged onto a flat open space. Directly in front of them, perched between two wind rounded mountains, stood Crown Peak. "Well, there it is," Quen said softly, staring at the flattened mountain peak.

Crown Peak was a lofty mountain with a flat, perfectly circular, summit. Equally spaced around the outer edge of the summit stood tall evenly cut massive square stone slabs giving it the appearance of a king's crown. Over the centuries legends sprang up to explain the mountain. Some said that ages past, before recorded history began, evil necromancers from the Isle of Naat had come to Cincor and had carved the great mountain peak thus, using it for horrible rites and rituals. Others said the mountain was where the great monster Nioth Korghai had alighted having come down from the sky. No matter the stories told to explain the past of Crown Peak, in the *here and now* the mountain had only one resident. The Wizard of Maraeva.

The travelers continued across the small open space and passed between the two rounded mountains that stood like sentinels before Crown Peak. The mountain loomed before them as they crossed onto a narrow path and began their ascent of Crown Peak. The ascent was slow and tedious on the narrow rock strewn path. Then, halfway up the mountainside, they came to a level plateau. The plateau was narrow, cut out of the mountainside.

Quen, Taum, Naura, and Isla peered around in shock, never having been to the lair of the old wizard. The plateau seemed to have been man made. Opposite the plateau's edge the mountain wall rose straight to the crowned peak. The wall of the mountain was curved, concave, looking as if it had been cut and shaped from the mountain rock. In the center of the curved wall was a cave entrance resembling an arched doorway. Framing the doorway were strange designs and symbols carved into the stone. On each side of the door were stone skulls with a third skull centered above the door. Next to the door, on the plateau, was a boulder which had been cut into the shape of a chair. Human footprints littered the dusty plateau.

"Well, we've found the right address," Taum chuckled, trying to alleviate his tension.

"It would seem so," Quen replied softly.

Quen cautiously dismounted. The others followed. Together they hesitated, peering with uncertainty at the cave entrance.

"I still wish you girls would have stayed home," Quen said suddenly. "This is no place for you."

"I wouldn't miss this for the world," Isla replied.

"Quen's right, you shouldn't have come," Taum said.

"Enough with the lectures," Naura said. "Are we going in?"

"Aye. Just a minute," Quen replied.

Quen turned to his camel and pulled his sabre and a dagger from their saddle scabbards. The sabre's three foot curved blade glinted brightly in the sunlight as Quen latched the ring on its' hilt to a catch on his belt. The dagger, with its snaked blade, he placed in his boot. The hilts of both dagger and sabre were made of white pearl inlaid with garnet stone in the shape of the letter 'Q'.

"I'm glad you brought those along," Taum said guardedly as Quen placed the dagger in his boot.

"The old sorcerer said something...a Geerla...," Quen began.

"You believe that?" Naura interrupted.

"Frankly I do," Quen replied, a fire in his eyes.

"Well, let's find out," Naura said brazenly, then turned and began to walk toward the cave entrance. Quen stared at her, shaking his head. She was beautiful, supple, with brown eyes and long black hair, but at times her brash attitude cast a dark pall over her attractive physical attributes. At the cave entrance Naura paused and glanced back. "Well, are you coming," she said from the cave entrance.

Quen glanced at Taum. "Get a torch," he said softly.

Taum nodded as he turned to his camel, pulling a three foot wooden staff from a pack. Attached to one end of the staff was a wrapping of cloth soaked in melted wax. Holding the torch up before him, Taum turned back to Quen.

There was a short pause, then Quen, Taum, and Isla approached the cave entrance where Naura stood waiting for them. With a cold glare at Naura, Quen led his companions into the darkened entrance. The cave abruptly curved to the right. In seconds Quen and his companions were plunged in darkness. Taum lit the torch and held it up to the cave walls. The walls were slimy and damp, green with a very thin layer of moss. The cave floor was wet, the dampness of the walls trickling to the floor.

They walked, Taum's torch cutting the thick dark like a knife. Quen and Taum were apprehensive, Isla wide-eyed, occasionally glancing over her shoulder certain that something was lurking behind them. But there was nothing, only the darkness they had already passed through. Naura was impatient, fearing nothing. She wanted to get to the heart of the matter, be it some strange old man that people called a wizard or some monstrous creature lurking in some mist that she really didn't believe in.

After what seemed hours the dark of the cave seemed to lessen. Ahead a soft blue light was glowing. The four young people paused, staring at the softly glowing light before them. Its' blue radiance glimmered like the flickering of a candle flame. The light seemed to be creeping along the cave walls, turning the green tinted walls to a dark dull shade of blue. Quen and his companions exchanged puzzled glances, then continued toward the source of the light.

Cautiously, they emerged in an underground cavern. The walls of the cavern emanated the soft blue radiance, illuminating the great stone chamber except for the ceiling which receded into the darkness high above. The cavern floor sloped downward in front of them. To each side the floor rose to become narrow walkways, skirting the cavern wall to the side opposite from where they stood. In the middle of the floor was a large pool with a thin layer of blue mist clinging to its surface. Cold blue flames danced off the water.

"The mist the old sorcerer spoke of," Taum said softly, staring at the pool.

"Aye," Quen replied.

"I don't see any horrible monster," Naura said.

Naura walked to the edge of the pool and peered to the other side. The mist swirled as the flames danced across the water. Looking through the flames and mist, Naura could see the narrow walkways merging to form a small platform. On the platform was another opening in the cavern wall leading deeper into the mountain.

"Don't get too close," Quen shouted to Naura.

"Don't worry, there's nothing...," Naura began, turning to Quen.

As Naura turned her back on the pool, a hissing cry resounded through the cavern. She turned back to the pool, her eyes wide. A succession of bubbles broke the surface, concentric rings fanning to the edge of the pool. A slithering green mass in the shape of a tentacle broke the water's edge, wrapping itself around Naura's ankle. And she screamed.

Sabre already in hand, Quen rushed to Naura's side and began to hack away at the tentacle. Green liquid oozed from the sabre cuts. Quen paused only long enough to catch a glimpse of the monstrous Geerla breaking the surface in the middle of the pool. Naura's scream alerted him to the amorphous jelly like mass coming out of the water, several tentacles writhing in the air. Side stepping a flying tentacle, Quen again began to hack away at the tentacle wrapped around Naura's ankle.

The monster began to pull back, taking Naura with it. The tentacle inched its' way into the pool, dragging Naura ever closer to the water. Naura dug her fingernails into the soft water soaked floor of the cavern as she continued to scream. There was no time to save her, no way the sabre would cut through the tentacle before it dragged Naura to her death beneath the water. With tears in his eyes, resigned to losing Naura, Quen slowly backed away.

"Release her, Geerla!" a commanding voice suddenly resounded from the other side of the pool. "They come as friends!"

Quen, Taum, and Isla glanced across the pool. A tall figure adorned in a plain floor length gray cloak stood on the platform. The figure was an old man, ancient, with long white hair and beard. At the sound of the old man's voice, Geerla released Naura and slipped beneath the surface of the pool. Naura picked herself up from the water's edge. She shuddered from fright and the cold water, then backed away from the pool, alternating glances between the pool and the old man on the platform.

"It's him!" Taum exclaimed as he and Isla joined Quen. "The Maraevan Wizard!"

"Aye," Quen said as Naura joined them.

"Come around!" the wizard shouted, gesturing to the walkway with a hand. "Follow the walkway around the pool. Do not be afraid; Geerla won't harm you."

"That's what you say," Naura thought softly aloud.

"Well, are you coming?" the old wizard questioned.

Slowly, their eyes on the old wizard, Quen and his companions followed the walkway around the pool to the platform where the old wizard stood. As they neared him they noticed the old wizard's age shown only in the color of his hair. His face was clear of age lines. A gleam of light shown in his eyes, foretelling of great wisdom.

"Welcome! Welcome!" the old wizard exclaimed as Quen and his companions mounted the platform. "I have been expecting you!"

3
The Maraevan Wizard

Three wall mounted torches bathed the cavern home of the old wizard in a soft light. The cavern walls were smooth, seemingly hand worked, and adorned with odd inscriptions and symbols, the like of which were known only to those who had use of them. The earthen floor, textured as the walls, was smooth and level. Along one wall ran a series of shelves supported by ivory legs with intricately carved bas-relief's. An old wooden trunk rested on the floor next to the shelves, its' lid carved with a strange inscription unknown to Quen and his companions.

In the middle of the floor was a large circular well, topped with a stone ring rising a foot above the level of the floor. In the well shimmered a blue liquid with color and texture very much like that of the pool where Geerla dwelt. To one side of the well rested a reclining lounger adorned with throw covers of satin and velvet. Behind the lounger, lining the wall opposite the trunk and shelves, rested several tall bookcases. The bookcases stood in disarray, books haphazardly piled on the shelves. Between the well and the ivory leg supported shelves stood a long rectangular wooden table with six chairs. Centered on the table was a single lit white candle.

The old wizard glanced at the candle, then shuffled past the table to a white cane leaning against the stone wall. Grasping the cane by its' handle which was carved in the shape of a human skull, the old wizard turned and shuffled to the well.

"Well, the time has been long since I've had visitors," the old wizard said as he shuffled past Quen and his companions who were standing at table. "The people of Maraeva...," he paused, shook his head, and chuckled. "Huh! The people of Cincor seem to have this grave misconception of me. They think I'm evil. I can't imagine why." The old wizard stopped at the well. He peered momentarily into the blue water, then turned to face Quen, Taum, Isla, and Naura. "I am Quaestor."

"I am Quen, and this is...," Quen began, gesturing to Naura.

"I know who you are," Quaestor interrupted. "I know all of you."

"You said you were expecting us," Taum said.

"All in due time," Quaestor replied, gesturing patience with a hand. "All in due time. I am not as agile as I use to be."

Slowly Quaestor began to circle the well of blue water. Gaining a position opposite Quen and his companions, Quaestor stopped and looked at the four young people. He grinned as he tapped the circular stone ring of the well with his cane. "This is the reason," Quaestor replied with a smile. "Through this I saw your coming."

"We came here to...," Quen began.

"You came here to learn of Maraeva's Shunned Quarter," Quaestor interrupted as he shuffled to the table. "Come and sit." The old wizard took a seat at the head of the table while Quen and his companions sat to each side of him. "You want to know the dark secrets, the mysteries. Maraeva's founder," Quaestor said softly after they had seated themselves at the table.

"Aye," Taum said softly, his eyes averted.

"Why come to me?" Quaestor asked after a pause for thought.

"An old sorcerer told us to seek you out," Quen replied.

"Old sorcerer?" Quaestor's eyes brightened as he leaned forward and nodded. "Ah, that would be Blacius, a one time apprentice of mine." He sat back, his eyes trained on infinity as he thought back on old times. Quaestor's eyes gleamed as he saw things Quen and his companions couldn't see, a truth they couldn't see. Then Quaestor surfaced from his reverie of the past and grinned at the four young people who sat at the table with him. "You came to ask me what Blacius could not answer," he said.

"Aye," Quen replied.

"Well, with that...," Quaestor began, turning in his chair and gesturing to the well with his cane. "I could show you many wonders, tell you tales of the Kingdom of Calyz, destroyed by Thasaidon's black cloak of death; of sacrifices made to Mordiggian, the god of death in Zul-Bha-Sair. I could tell you the legends of Nioth Korghai coming from the sky...," Quaestor suddenly fell silent. Slowly he leaned over the table and continued, his voice a whisper, "Or I could tell you things that are not yet, but shall be...things such as the Silver Death that will come in the night and lay waste to Tasuun and Yoros, or of the great city of Ummaos which shall be destroyed by the necromancy of Namirrha."

"Just the Shunned Quarter," Quen interrupted mildly. "That's what we want to know about."

"Aye," Quaestor resigned as he sat back. "The Shunned Quarter. The Shunned Quarter in Maraeva arose many centuries ago soon after Maraeva was founded. Maraeva's Founder gave rise to the Shunned Quarter after dabbling in black necromancy."

"Aye, that we already know," Taum said.

"Aye, Blacius, then come and look into my well," Quaestor said.

Grasping his cane for support, Quaestor rose from the table and shuffled to the well. Quen and his companions followed. Quaestor passed his cane over the water, and an image began to form. At first hazy, the image began to clear until a barren landscape could be seen. Looming close by in the image was a great stone altar with stone pillars towering to each side. Near the altar walked a small white goat. In the distance were the small mud huts of Maraeva in an earlier time.

Suddenly the black cloaked Founder appeared in the image. His hood was drawn up, his face concealed. The Founder approached the goat, reached down and patted its head, then approached the stone altar. In his hand he carried a long crooked staff of wood.

"That which you see, the barren landscape and the altar are where the Shunned Quarter of Maraeva stands today," Quaestor said as the Founder neared the altar.

"What is he doing?" Naura asked.

"Wait and you shall see," Quaestor replied.

The Founder stopped before the altar, his back to those peering at the image. After a moment's hesitation the Founder raised his staff to the sky with both hands. In the image dark clouds suddenly rolled across the sky. The wind grew wild, lightning flashing from the darkening clouds. A great bolt of blue lightning erupted from the churning clouds, striking the end of the staff. The staff began to glow with a blue light, extending down the entire length of the staff to the Founder's hands. As the blue light faded, so did the clouds and wind.

"That is how it began," Quaestor said softly. "The beginning of the darkness that would descend upon Maraeva, and give rise to the Shunned Quarter."

"The lightning should have killed him!" Isla exclaimed.

"Any normal man or woman would have been killed," Quaestor sighed. "But the Founder wasn't a normal man. It was the dark arts that made him as you see."

"But it still doesn't tell us anything," Naura said.

"What do you want it to tell you?" Quaestor said. Gesturing to the well, the old wizard added, "Watch and see."

All eyes turned to the well once again. The Founder stepped away from the altar. The light of day and wispy clouds had once again returned to the skies of ancient Maraeva. The Founder walked slowly to the goat that was still standing nearby. He held out a hand.

The goat peered up at the Founder. There was terror in the goat's eyes. The goat stiffened, its eyes glazing over, then suddenly toppled over on its side. It kicked its hind legs twice, then it was still. And the Founder slowly lowered his hand to his side.

"He killed it!" Naura exclaimed.

"Aye," Quaestor said softly.

Silence descended in the cavern as Quen and his companions stared into the well. Quaestor remained silent, studying the four young people. There was torment on their faces, bewilderment in their eyes. It had been a display of the Founder's power, the same power which gave rise to the dark mysteries and terrors that had formed the foundation of the Shunned Quarter.

Quaestor passed his cane over the well. The image dissolved, the blue water taking on its original texture and color. The four young people stared in silence at the blue water as if the image was still there. Quaestor turned away, and shuffled back to the table. Lines of thought were furrowed deep on Quaestor's forehead. *Would destiny be fulfilled?* Quaestor wondered. *Should I try to stop it?* Quaestor knew the fate of Maraeva rested in his hands, and that fate, that destiny, was close at hand.

"If only he could have been stopped," Quen said softly, still staring at the blue water of the well.

Quaestor glanced at Quen. His left eyebrow was arched, a grin spreading across his face. "If he could have been? What then?" the old wizard said as he slowly approached the well. "I have thought the same. Yet, I conclude that fate cannot be changed. History cannot be changed. Or denied." Quaestor fell silent. He cocked his head to one side and gently smiled at the lie behind his words.

Quen glanced at Quaestor. There had been something in the old wizard's voice. It was more than a question that Quaestor had just proposed. There was a hidden meaning. Quen was certain. Perhaps it was a challenge. Whatever was behind the words of the old wizard, the four of the young people had noted the mystery.

Quaestor tapped the edge of the well with his cane. "It is one thing to talk of the horrors of the past," he said, staring into the blue water. "It is quite another to experience it." He turned his cane up under an arm, then gazed at Quen, and grinned. "You can, you know. Experience it."

"How?" Quen asked.

"By traveling to the past," Quaestor replied.

"Impossible!" Isla exclaimed. "No one can travel in time!"

Quaestor smiled, his eyes brightening. "Quite to the contrary, it IS possible."

A playing-the-hero thought came over Quen. He turned away from the others, his mind racing with thoughts of traveling to Maraeva's beginning. *Traveling to the past.* Quen's curiosity raced with expectancy. *Think of it! To travel to the past!* Quen stared blindly at the cavern wall, his eyes distant. *To confront the Founder, nae...to STOP the Founder... The Shunned Quarter would disappear forever.* Quen smiled at the thought.

Quaestor smiled as well, his eyes trained on Quen. The seed had been sown. The game would be played out. The fate of Maraeva would be settled. Maraeva would continue to exist. All that Quen had to do was travel to the past. Quaestor was certain that Quen would never pass up the chance for youth's desire was too great. And Quaestor knew it.

Quen turned his eyes to Quaestor. "Can you send me back?"

"Aye, but...," Quaestor began.

"Then I can stop the founder!" Quen interrupted. "The Shunned Quarter need never arise! I can alter history!"

"History cannot be changed," Quaestor said, knowing in his mind that it could. "Or denied."

"If I go back, I can stop him," Quen insisted. "If I stop him, history is changed."

"All right," Quaestor began, playing into his own lie. "If you need to see for yourself that history cannot be changed... Follow me."

Quen followed the old wizard to a dark alcove in the wall. The alcove was virtually concealed in shadows where the torch light could not penetrate. Quaestor stopped before the alcove, gesturing Quen to step inside.

"Quen!" Naura exclaimed, running to him. "You can't..."

"I can," Quen interrupted. "Naura...I must."

Naura fought for something to say, but could not. In frustration tears came to her eyes. "You must play the hero!" she finally blurted out. "Why not let someone else?"

"Please Naura, trust me," Quen said from the alcove then smiled.

"All right," Naura sobbed. Her eyes on Quen, Naura slowly backed away toward the well. She didn't want to see him go, an inner feeling telling her she would never see him again. For a moment Quen's heart wavered. Just as quickly his heart hardened. Quen glanced at Quaestor then at Taum.

"Take care of her for me until I return," Quen said softly.

"Aye," Taum said softly as he and Isla slowly stepped forward to comfort Naura.

Quaestor lowered his head, then turned to Quen in the alcove. The time had finally come. Quaestor wondered if he shouldn't tell Quen the truth. But if Quen knew, what then? Perhaps Quen would stay. If so, Maraeva would cease to exist, and all who lived there, all who had ever lived in Maraeva, would cease to be.

"Know this for it is the truth," Quaestor said, his voice wavering. "You shall never come face to face with the Founder."

"I must try," Quen replied.

There was a moment of silence as Quaestor glanced at Quen's companions. They stood in silence at the well, watching and waiting. Then Quaestor turned back to Quen.

"Are you ready?" Quaestor asked.

"Aye," Quen replied.

"You see the gemstones on each side of the alcove," Quaestor said. "Place your hands on them. The stones will transport you."

Quaestor stepped back. Quen glanced at the gemstones embedded in the alcove then rested his hands on them. Immediately they began to glow, a soft red light filling the alcove. Quen could feel a warmth coming from the stones, their light glistening off the white pearl hilt of Quen's sabre. Suddenly Quen began to fade. Then he was gone. The light of the gemstones began to soften, then fade.

"Destiny has been fulfilled," Quaestor said softly. He turned and shuffled slowly toward Taum, Isla, and Naura.

At Quaestor's words a sudden fear crept into Taum. Naura, her eyes questioning, glanced at the old wizard. Quaestor remained silent as he stopped before the well, tapping his cane on its edge. Taum, Naura, and Isla turned to the well.

"Destiny fulfilled?" Taum questioned softly.

Quaestor remained silent as he passed his cane over the well once again. Another image began to form, then cleared. They peered upon a street in the Shunned Quarter of an earlier Maraeva. Death and misery lined the streets. Strange malformed creatures shuffled in and out of the shadows. Cloaked necromancers came and went. Then the Founder appeared, walking slowly along the street, his hood still drawn up. All the wretched creatures in the street scrambled out of his way.

"History cannot be changed," Quaestor said softly. "Your friend had to go to the past."

A sudden thought struck Taum. He hoped he was wrong, but the old wizard's cryptic words seemed to weigh heavy on his mind. There was an answer to a question that had plagued he and Quen ever since talking with Blacius in Maraeva, a question they, for some reason, had neglected to ask Quaestor thus far. And Taum knew that Quaestor had the answer.

"Blacius said you know who the Founder was," Taum said softly, voicing the question as a statement.

Quaestor paused. He glanced at Taum. There was sadness in the old wizard's eyes. "Aye, I know." Quaestor turned his sad eyes back to the well. Taum and the two girls followed his gaze. "Observe," Quaestor said, pointing to the image.

They watched Founder walk along the street then crossed into a square and came to a stop next to the altar the four young people had seen earlier. The Founder paused, then turned. He reached up, pulled back the hood of his cloak, and revealed his face. Quaestor looked at the face passively, sadly. Taum and the girls stood aghast. Taum shook his head; his guess had been right. Isla stared open mouthed, wide eyed. Naura shook with fear as she gazed upon the countenance of the Founder.

"It can't be!" Naura's voice breaking. "It just can't be!"

"It is," Quaestor replied softly, still gazing at the image.

Naura fell to her knees, burying her face in her hands.

4
The Founder

Quaestor, Taum, and the two girls sat quietly at the great wooden table. The candle on the table flickered, the dancing flame catching Taum's eyes. He glanced at the flame; his eyes saw only the face of the Founder. And Taum realized the destiny Quaestor had spoken of. Yet, there were still many unanswered questions.

"So the Founder was Quen," Taum said casually.

"Aye. Quen, the Founder of Maraeva and the Shunned Quarter," Quaestor replied, glancing at Taum.

"You've got to bring him back!" Naura pleaded. Her eyes were red with tears.

"Impossible," Quaestor replied. "It cannot be done."

"Why not?" Taum asked. "You sent him there!"

Quaestor rose from the table. "There is more to it than you realize," he replied.

Taum watched as Quaestor shuffled to the well and stared into the blue water. Taum could tell that the old wizard was thinking, but he didn't know what was on the old wizard's mind. Taum glanced at Naura and Isla, then rose from the table and approached Quaestor. Hands in his pockets, Taum stared at the blue water in the well for a moment, then looked at the old wizard.

"What else is there to it?" Taum said softly.

Quaestor shook his head as he glanced at Taum. There was a strange light in the old wizard's eyes. Taum noted remorse, a sadness. In that moment Taum knew that this old man, this wizard so long misrepresented, couldn't hurt anyone.

"I am sorry, but nothing can be changed," Quaestor said sadly.

"What about Quen?" Taum asked.

"He is where he is suppose to be," Quaestor replied. "You must understand. Quen founded Maraeva. Without Quen in the past, there would be no Maraeva. It is a matter of history, a history which has already been written."

Taum turned from the well, threw his hands into the air in despair and disbelief. He walked a few steps toward the table, then turned to face Quaestor again. "There has to be a way around this! Quen belongs here, in this time. He was born into this time!"

Quaestor turned slowly to face Taum. The light still shown in his eyes, but still shadowed by sadness. Quaestor read the distress in Taum's voice, saw it in Taum's eyes. "There is no way around it. Quen had to travel into the past to set a course of action that would bring about the Maraeva we have today," Quaestor replied softly. "In effect, he has many times before. Maraeva, you, I, the girls - we exist. Maraeva WAS founded. Quen is proof of that. We are flesh, and blood, and bone..." Quaestor paused, glanced at the old wooden chest, then back at Taum. "Let me show you something that should interest you very much."

Quaestor shuffled past Taum to the old wooden chest near the shelves. He stared at the lid for a moment, then flung back the latch and opened it. Quaestor sorted through the contents, lifting an object from the trunk that immediately caught the eyes of Taum and the two girls. It was an ancient sabre.

The old wizard turned, drew his cane up under an arm and held the ancient sabre up with both hands. He grinned at Taum. The youth approached, his eyes locked on the ancient weapon. He gasped, eyes wide, in disbelief. The sabre showed great age – crusty, fragile, tarnished. Its' blade was rusted and notched from use. The hilt was tarnished, yet easily recognizable, made of white pearl inlaid with a red letter Q.

"This sabre belonged to an ancestor of mine," Quaestor said softly. "My name is Quaestor Quondam. I am a blood descendent of Quen. People know me to be a wizard. That is true for it courses in my blood, a heritage begun by Quen Quondam."

"But I don't...," Taum began in disbelief.

"Naura!" Isla shouted, cutting Taum short.

Quaestor and Taum turned. Isla was wide eyed, rising from the table, watching as Naura ran to the alcove. Quaestor pointed a finger, arms length, at Naura as the young woman stepped into the alcove.

"You know not what you do, young lady!" Quaestor called to her. "You don't know how far back in time he has..."

"I don't care!" Naura interrupted, tears in her eyes. "Quen's back there and I'm going back to get him."

"Naura, Quaestor is right, you don't know when…," Taum began.

"I'll find him," Naura interrupted, her voice breaking.

She placed her hands on the gemstones. The red light began to glow, filtering into the cavern then began to fade. Naura was gone, emptiness and shade once again pervading the alcove.

Quaestor shook his head. "She doesn't know what she's done."

"What can we do?" Taum said.

"Nothing, I'm afraid," Quaestor replied, shuffling to the table. The old wizard laid the sabre on the table, then glanced at Taum and Isla. "Come."

Quaestor shuffled back to the well. Taum and Isla followed. The wizard passed his cane over the well. The blue water shimmered and another image formed. It was dusk, night coming. The view was the small square in the Shunned Quarter, the square with the stone altar. A crowd of evil necromancers and the lawless were gathered. A ritual was underway with a column of necromancers holding flaming torches, the flames dancing in the darkening sky. The crowd was chanting and dancing at a feverish pitch. Shadows writhed across the scene. The dancing suddenly stopped. The crowd, gathered around the stone altar, began to part as the tall black cloaked figure of a middle aged Quen stepped toward the altar. For the first time Quaestor, Taum, and Isla could see the altar plainly. Shackled to the altar, spread eagle, lay Naura, her eyes wide with terror.

Quaestor, Taum, and Isla watched as Quen stopped at the altar and raised a hand. The chanting seemed to have stopped. Quen drank from a goblet that had been passed to him. There was terror in Naura's eyes as she peered up at the middle aged Quen. Quen reached down, tore open her blouse then produced a dagger from the folds of his cloak. *His snake bladed dagger*, Taum noted. Quaestor, Taum, and Isla watched in horror as Quen raised the dagger over his head, paused then plunged it into Naura's chest.

Quaestor passed his cane over the well once again. The image vanished. He lowered his head as he shuffled away from the well. Taum continued to stare into the well. All he saw was blue water. Isla turned her head, watching the old wizard.

"He killed her," Isla said softly, tears flowing.

Quaestor stopped, turning to Taum and Isla. Taum looked at him. For the first time Taum and Isla saw the physical expression of sorrow on Quaestor's face. He, like Isla, had tears in his eyes.

"Aye, he did," Quaestor replied softly.

*   *   *

Naura shifted to one side, leaning on an elbow, and wiped sweat from her forehead. "Sweat," she laughed under her breath. *Aye, sweat. What had they called it? A sweat hut? For purification? Purification for what?* It was hot in the sweat hut, glowing coals beneath the floor making the small cramped thatched hut almost unbearably hot. Her cloths were ringing wet. Her face was soiled, bruised from the beatings. Her ribs pained. She gazed at the bruise on her right forearm, winced at the pain in her back then shifted her position again. It was hard to get comfortable in the cramped hut.

The hut was completely enclosed. A leather flap acted as a door. There was no way out. The hut was guarded. Naura had been out of the hut twice since they put her in it. Both times were for the beatings she had undergone. Naura had no idea how long she had been confined to the hut, only that it had been a very long time. She was weak from the beatings and from not having been fed. She had pleaded to see Quen, and had been told that she would see him soon. That was a consolation. At least he was there, somewhere. He would set things right. He would get her out of this.

The leather flap flew open. Two men entered. Naura glanced at them. There was fear in her eyes. *Another beating?* She wondered. The two men glared at her as they dragged her to her feet. They shoved her toward the entrance of the hut. She stumbled into the soft light of dusk, shielding her eyes which had been accustomed to the continual darkness of the hut.

The two men waited, letting Naura's eyes adjust to the light. Slowly she lowered her hand and gazed around. It was the same small village of dilapidated mud huts, but this time something was different. Naura wasn't sure what was different, only that she could sense it. There were noises of revelry, screams of pain, laughter, shouts, and barking dogs. Smoke rose from alleys above the roofs of the village. *Maraeva. The Shunned Quarter.* Naura shook her head.

She glanced back at the two men. They pointed toward an alley that led into the cluster of mud huts. Naura turned, following the direction they were pointing. Standing at the entrance of an alley she noted a column of black cloaked figures carrying lighted torches. The flames of the torches danced on the encroaching night air. Suddenly, one of the men pushed her forward.

"I'm not going anywhere until I see Quen," Naura voiced, trying to feign anger in her weakened state.

"You will do as you are told," one of the men replied angrily. "You will see Lord Quandom soon."

Naura remained silent. She turned and walked toward the column of cloaked figures. The two men followed. Naura and the two men joined the column and turned into the alley. The alley was lined with the squalid mud huts, their doors opened on shadows. Naura glanced from one side of the alley to the other. Evil and lawlessness were gathered there. She saw necromancers, evil lecherous men, old hags, witches, and harlots. They taunted and laughed. They threw stones, mud, and rotten fruit at her. Some of the men squeezed her, pinched her, prodded her with lewd and malicious intent as she was led toward an unknown destination. Old hags ran to her, pulled her hair and cackled. The procession continued deeper into the cluster of mud huts. Those clamoring in the doorways and shadows fell in behind the two men, following the procession to its destination. Finally the column of torch bearers came to an open square. They circled to the right. Naura entered the square and saw for the first time the great stone altar she had seen in the images of Quaestor's well.

The stone altar was in the center of the square. It was a large oblong altar, black in color, rough cut with strange symbols carved on it, symbols she hadn't noticed in the images she had seen. The column of torch bearers circled the altar, then formed a double row opposite from where they had entered the square. Walking between the two rows of torch bearers the two men led Naura to the altar. Naura noticed the chain shackles anchored at the four corners of the altar. In the deepening purple of twilight she also noted the dark red stains that covered the top of the altar, stains of something that had poured down the sides of the altar to the dusty earthen square. *Blood,* her mind screamed. *Sacrificial blood.*

"No!" Naura screamed as the two men grabbed and pulled her toward the altar. "No! Leave me alone! Where's Quen?"

Her struggled was in vain. She was backhanded, the stinging blow causing Naura to regain her composure enough to stare in disbelief at the man who had struck her. The man simply laughed. Naura was lifted atop the altar and placed on her back. She began to whimper as they shackled her, spread-eagle, in the wrist and ankle cuffs. The crowd that followed the procession into the square began to gather around the altar. The two men stepped back, standing side by side in front of the double row of torch bearers.

Chanting began. The chatter of the crowd diminished as the chanting took precedence. Naura peered about wildly. She saw faces leering at her, faces of evil, sparkling eyes of madness, heaving breath of bloodlust awaiting bloodshed. Dancing began, building to a frenzy. The torch flames danced on the darkening night. Naura closed her eyes, wanting it to stop, hoping it was a dream. She opened them. The horror was still there. She called out for Quen. Quen didn't answer. *A ceremony*, her mind cried out. *I'm a sacrifice!*

Still whimpering, Naura peered up at the sky. She remembered those points of light in the sky were called stars; she had read about them in an old book. Night coming on fast. She shook her head and turned her eyes back to the torch bearers. The flames continued to dance against the darkening sky. The chanting reached a feverish pitch. The frenzied dancing had taken the form of concentric rings revolving around the stone altar. Suddenly the dancing stopped. The crowd began to part, the dancing rings broken. Someone was approaching. Naura strained her neck to see who it was.

Quen, in his long black cloak, stepped to the altar. He peered down at the prone figure of Naura. There was no trace of recognition in his eyes, eyes which sparkled in an evil light. Naura peered at his face, a face showing middle age, a gray tint to his hair, lines on his face. And she realized she had lost him. Any trace of goodness that had once been Quen had long been gone. This man was Quen, it was true, but not the Quen that Naura had once known.

Naura's eyes remained locked on the Quen she didn't know, her eyes wide with terror. Quen raised a hand. The chanting softened, then stopped. A deathly silence descended on the square. A hooded figure handed Quen a goblet. He drank from the goblet, then handed it back to the hooded figure. Naura looked up at him wide eyed, uncertain, terror racking her frame in shivers.

"Quen?" she said, her voice soft, almost inaudible.

Quen ignored her. He reached down, tore open the fabric of her blouse. From the folds of his cloak he produced a dagger, the snake bladed dagger he had brought with him to Quaestor's cavern home. The pearl handle was yellowed with age. He grasped the dagger with both hands, and raised it over his head. Everyone waited. Naura stared in terror at the raised blade. She knew what was going to happen. Quen wasn't going to save her. He was the instrument of her death.

The blade descended. In one last fleeting moment she pictured the cavern home of Quaestor, heard Quaestor's voice softly in her mind telling her that she didn't know what she was doing. *You were right, you were right,* her mind cried. The image vanished in a scream of pain as the snake bladed dagger plunged deep into her breast. In involuntary reaction she pushed up against the dagger, then slowly settled down on the altar. Darkness came, and Naura was dead. Quen smiled, an evil gleam sparkling in his eyes.

5

The End of the Beginning

Taum and Isla sat staring at one another across the table. At one end of the table sat Quaestor, his cane leaning against the table, the ancient sabre lying before him. All were quiet, in deep reflection of the last image they had seen in the well. Isla turned her eyes to the table top, occasionally shaking her head in disbelief. The only sound was that of Taum tapping his fingers on the table. He glanced at the ancient sabre that had been Quen's, then at Quaestor.

Quaestor ran his fingers lightly over the tarnished hilt of the sabre. In his mind he played the image of Naura on the stone altar, the image of her death at the hands of Quen. It was an image he had never before seen in the well. Of course, he had never looked for it. Naura's death, if in fact it was part of history, would have been a minor event. Easily overlooked. Quaestor shook his head. *A minor event?* He couldn't be sure.

"I just can't believe this," Isla thought aloud, breaking the silence. "Quen killed her."

"If I could go back to a time before Naura's death...," Taum began, dwelling on the possibility.

"It doesn't matter...," Quaestor said, interrupting Taum.

"How can you say that?" Isla glared at Quaestor.

"I am as saddened as you at the death of your young friend," Quaestor said. Turning to Taum, he added: "You have to understand. There are no guarantees going into the past."

"I've got to try," Taum said, finally convincing himself.

"You take grave risks," Quaestor said. "You don't know what time period you will find yourself in. It was your young lady friend's misfortune to find Quen in the period in which she did."

"But if I can go back before that time and bring Quen back...," Taum began.

"Bring Quen back?" Quaestor interrupted. "I exist, and this sword, and Maraeva! It is proof Quen lived in the past. Quen belongs to the past. He cannot be brought back. It is a fact of time, a fact of history, a fact that cannot be changed."

Cannot be changed. The words echoed in Taum's mind as a sudden thought arose. Blacius had said only the Founder could take away the darkness of the Shunned Quarter. Quen could change the past, but he had to be made to realize that the past had to be changed. Someone had to tell Quen. Taum knew he had to try. For the sake of Naura, for the sake of Quen, for the sake of Maraeva. *Cannot be changed*, he reflected. *I'll just have to take that chance.*

Taum suddenly turned and glanced toward the alcove where Quen had stood before he had disappeared into the past. Fear crept into his soul. Taum wondered what control he would have, when in the past he would arrive, or if he would even find Quen. It didn't really matter. Without another thought Taum rose from the table and approached the alcove then glanced back at Isla and Quaestor. Isla peered back questioningly. Quaestor understood. He knew.

"It won't work," Quaestor said softly.

"How do you know it won't?"

"I know," Quaestor replied. "The past cannot be changed. Or denied."

"I've got to try," Taum replied.

"The same words Quen had spoken," Quaestor said softly.

The phrase caught Taum off guard. For a moment he stared at Quaestor then shrugged it off and glanced at Isla. Taum smiled at her then entered the alcove. He placed his hands on the two gemstones. They began to glow. Taum glanced around the cavern room. The red glow of the gemstones blurred his vision. The room began to fade. Objects became translucent, hazy, ghost-like. Then the room was gone. His mind reeled in darkness.

* * *

Taum opened his eyes, and found himself lying on his back. Above him was a blue sky dotted with white puffy clouds. He struggled to his feet, his legs wobbly. He gazed around, taking in the bleak rocky landscape of a parched and desolate land. And Taum began to wonder if he had been wrong in coming backward in time.

He had no idea of where he was in time or if Quen existed in the time he now found himself. Perhaps Quen lay in his future, perhaps the past. Taum's thoughts began to drift. He wondered what his own presence in the past meant, if it had changed anything, perhaps caused some irreparable damage to the time line. Most important on his mind was how he was going to get back home to his own time.

"Taum! What are you doing here?" the voice came from behind.

Taum spun on his heels, his legs nearly giving out. He knew the voice. Taum's fears suddenly vanished. He stared up at Quen and smiled. Quen stood atop a cluster of boulders, hands on his hips, smiling; the same Quen who only minutes earlier had left the cavern. Quen the dark necromancer still lay in the future. Taum knew there was still time. He watched as Quen climbed down from the cluster of boulders, then jump the last couple of feet to the ground.

Quen smiled, patting Taum on the shoulder. "So, what are you doing here?" he repeated.

"I've something to tell you," Taum said. You'd better sit down."

The two sat. Taum glanced at Quen, noted an eagerness in Quen's eyes. He paused a moment, deciding whether he should tell Quen of Naura's death. And for the first time Taum noted soft age lines around Quen's eyes and a faint trace of gray in Quen's hair.

Taum shrugged it off. After a short pause, he began to tell Quen the sketchy facts that Quaestor had related after Quen's departure. Quen listened with interest, never interrupting Taum's narrative.

"Quite a story," Quen said after Taum had finished, Taum having evaded Naura's death. "Aye, quite a story."

"Well, you've got to understand the Shunned Quarter exists because of you," Taum said.

"I find it kind of hard to believe...," Quen began.

"Maybe so, but I saw you in the image," Taum interrupted. "There's no doubt about it, Quen. You are the Founder."

"Well, I did find the altar," Quen said. He turned, gestured with a hand. "Over there. Below that craggy rise."

"You've found it? Taum asked. "You've only been gone a few minutes!"

"Seems longer," Quen replied. "Time displacement I suppose. A few minutes can be relative to days or centuries."

"I suppose so," Taum replied, sorting out the time question.

"I'll show you the altar," Quen said, rising to his feet.

Taum rose and followed Quen across the cluster of boulders from which he had appeared. The rocky rise, jagged with outcroppings of rock on the far side of the cluster, trailed away to an open clearing over a hundred feet below, the clearing itself ringed with rocks and pinnacles. And at one end of the clearing stood the stone altar.

They began their descent to the clearing. Taum glanced over his shoulder at the altar in the distance. A sudden movement caught Taum's eyes from above as he turned his attention to the wall of the rocky rise. Taum glanced up. A goat was standing on a rocky ledge looking down. For an instant Taum thought he could read a mocking laughter in the goat's eyes as if it knew something neither he nor Quen knew or could ever know.

Taum paused as he studied the goat then turned his eyes from it as he continued to descend the rise. The journey was hazardous, the jagged outcroppings, loose slag, and rocks littering the steep incline. Holding on to an outcropping, Taum looked down, searching for a place to rest a foot before descending another step. Below him was Quen. As Taum found a foothold, Quen looked up at him.

"Be careful," Quen yelled. "You can lose your footing."

"Aye," Taum replied, panting with physical exertion.

Then it happened. Quen rested his foot on loose slag. Shifting his weight, the world spun around before his eyes. The slag had shifted under his weight, throwing him off balance. Bouncing off boulders, Quen tumbled toward the clearing below.

"Quen!" Taum shouted, clinging to the rise wall. He watched in horror as Quen fell to the clearing below.

Taum stood frozen, clinging to the rise wall, peering down at Quen lying crumpled at the edge of the clearing. Quen didn't move. If Quen were dead, the full impact on the course of history hadn't registered in Taum's mind.

Taum suppressed his fear and uncertainty, and continued down the rock wall, quickening his descent still aware of needed caution. Taum repeatedly glanced over his shoulder at the prone figure of Quen lying far below. In his mind he kept telling Quen to move, to get up, but Quen wasn't listening. Quen remained still. *Unconscious. Only unconscious. Nothing to worry about. You'll be all right.*

Several minutes later and Taum was at the bottom of the rise. Jumping the last couple of feet to the clearing, he turned and ran to where Quen lay. He knelt over Quen, checked for a heartbeat, for breathing. He rolled Quen over, noted the trickle of blood from the corner of Quen's mouth, and checked again. Realization set in as a sudden cold chill gripped him. Taum slowly sat back and turned his eyes to the sky. He was alone.

"Quen!" Taum screamed.

Taum rose to his feet and wandered blindly into the clearing. He lost sense of time and place, left the clearing and wandered aimlessly among the crags. The sun set. The deep purple of dusk set in. He cursed Blacius for sending them down this path. He cursed Quen for stubbornly following the path. At one point he thought he saw the goat standing above him on a rocky ledge. Its eyes shown with an eerie light. Taum picked up a rock, threw it at the goat, then tore away from its' gaze.

Lost and hearing voices, the dark brought ghosts and visions to Taum. Time shifted, playing out the past, present, and future before his eyes, in his mind. He stopped, planted his feet firmly, and peered around. *Mad? Am I mad?* He cackled at the thought. *Time...change. Changing?* His mind a myriad of disjointed images, Taum sat and began to laugh as the voices echoed in his mind.

In his delusion he saw images of Zothique. He saw the past – the coming of the great Nioth Korghai; the fall of the Kingdom of Calyz as Thasaidon spread his black cloak of death across the land. He saw his present – the desert village of Maraeva; the Shunned Quarter; the face of Isla smiling at him. He saw the future – the Silver Death descending from Achernar; the destruction of Ummaos in Xylac by the phantom demon steeds of the necromancer Namirrha; and a bleak pestilence spread south across Cincor, leaving death and silence.

"Cincor, Maraeva, Zo...Zothique," Taum laughed aloud, forcing the names.

Amidst the voices his mind began to decay. Taum glanced up at the stars. He laughed again, his sanity dwindling, inching down a long black corridor. He rose to his feet, turned, and began to walk in a direction he couldn't remember. Taum realized that some thing or someone had told him to come this way, directing his path. Suddenly the many voices echoing in his mind became a single voice.

"History has been denied," the voice whispered in Taum's mind.

"Who are...who are...you," Taum whispered uncertainly.

"Thasaidon," came the simple reply.

"Thasaidon," Taum echoed softly. Voicing his thoughts, he added: "Huh. Lord of the Seven Hells."

Taum laughed as he peered into the sky, smiling at the twinkling stars. *So long ago, and yet, still to come.* He frowned, not knowing where the thought came from, then shook it off. He turned and unknowingly found himself back where he had first arrived in the desolate lands of Cincor's ancient past, the desolate land where Maraeva was yet to be founded. He didn't know how he had come to be there. He peered around expecting to hear Quen's voice again coming to him from the cluster of boulders above. But Quen's voice never came. Taum remembered that Quen lay dead somewhere, that Quen's voice would never come to him again.

"I want to go back!" Taum cried out. Again he turned his eyes to the black sky of night. "I don't belong here!"

"So you shall," the voice of Thasaidon whispered in his mind.

A red light began to glow about his feet. Taum looked down, his eyes wide. The light rose about him, enveloping him. The desolate landscape under the dark of night began to fade. He closed his eyes, paused then opened them. He found himself back in the alcove of Quaestor's cavern home. Isla was seated at the table. Quaestor stood by the old trunk, holding Quen's sabre. Taum met their gazes, and they saw the sadness in Taum's eyes as he stepped from the alcove.

"It's only been a few minutes," Isla said. "What happened?"

Taum shot a glance at her, but didn't reply. He caught movement out of the corner of his eyes, and turned to see Quaestor approaching. The old wizard laid the sabre on the table as he passed. "Well?" Quaestor said softly, his eyes questioning.

"He fell," Taum muttered, his voice breaking. "He fell."

"He fell?" the voice was Naura's.

Quaestor, Taum, and Isla turned; their eyes locked on Naura in disbelief. Naura was standing by the line of bookcases, apparently no worse for wear, no visible trace of the tattered and beaten condition she had exhibited in the images. She noted the surprised expressions of Quaestor, Taum, and Isla, expressions that puzzled her. She glanced between the three of them as Isla rose haltingly from the table and approached her.

"You said he fell," Naura said.

"Naura?" Isla questioned softly. "You've come back. How?"

Naura turned to Isla. "What are you talking about? I haven't been anywhere."

Taum stepped toward her. "We saw you..."

"No matter, no matter," Quaestor interrupted. "What is important is what happened to Quen." Quaestor shuffled to Taum and placed a nervous hand on the youth's shoulder. Taum glanced at him. "You said he fell," Quaestor echoed Naura's words.

"Aye," Taum replied softly.

"And?" Quaestor asked.

"Quen's dead," Taum replied sadly.

Quaestor looked away, his eyes downcast. Naura's sobs broke the momentary silence.

"That explains why Naura doesn't remember," Quaestor said, glancing at Taum.

"I don't understand," Taum said.

"Quen died before Naura was killed," Quaestor answered. "Her death never occurred."

"Killed?" Naura was incredulous.

"Aye, you were killed," Isla replied softly, Naura staring wide-eyed at her. "When you went after Quen…"

"I never left…," Naura began.

"When did he die?" Quaestor suddenly interrupted, terror evident in his voice, his eyes suddenly growing wide. A strange feeling had come over him. Quaestor was astonished. He clutched his stomach as he turned slowly to face Taum. In that instant his astonishment suddenly changed to visible terror. "Come now, boy, tell me!"

"Back there," Taum replied. "Back in time."

"Aye, aye!" Quaestor said, shaking his head. "At what point in his life? How old was he?"

"Well, like he was here; perhaps a little older" Taum said. "Not like we saw him in the…"

"Come!" Quaestor shouted, interrupting Taum.

Quaestor turned to the cavern entrance. Taum, Naura, and Isla followed. They hurriedly left the cavern, passed Geerla's pool, and headed for the mountainside entrance. They emerged from the mountain onto the narrow plateau. Quaestor stopped and was joined by Taum and the girls. They glanced at him questioningly. The old wizard's eyes were turned to Maraeva in the distance.

"What is it?" Taum asked, a sudden strange feeling coursing through him.

"Look!" Quaestor exclaimed, pointing to Maraeva.

Taum and the girls looked. Surprise tugged at their eyes. Maraeva seemed to shimmer in the evening sun. The city appeared ghostlike, faded. Taum thought it a trick of the setting sun. *A dust and sand storm; sun light refraction.* Taum tried to convince himself. He shook his head, unconvinced.

"What's happening to Maraeva?" Taum asked as the shimmering city seemed to fade before their eyes.

"Don't you understand?" Quaestor asked.

Taum glanced at Quaestor. Fear and wonder rose in Taum's soul. Quaestor was now shimmering, transparent, ghostlike – just like Maraeva. It was no trick of the setting sun; no dust clouds. Taum turned to the girls, finding them ghostlike as well.

"Quen is dead," Quaestor said suddenly, his voice a whisper, ethereal. "Maraeva was never founded."

"That's why Naura came back," Isla said. "She never died."

"Aye...," Quaestor replied. He paused, a final despair falling upon him, then added softly, "And we were never born. History has been denie..."

The word vanished with Quaestor. And one by one Taum, Isla, and Naura also disappeared as they watched Maraeva fade away. Silence descended on the narrow plateau niched into the side of Crown Peak. The wind whistled softly across the plateau and into the cave opening. The cave opening was rough, uneven. The strange carvings and skulls marking the entrance were gone. Or rather, they had never come to be.

Night fell over the barren plain where Maraeva had once been. Brush rolled across the windswept plain in the darkness. Little whirlpools of dust scurried about then disappeared into endless oblivion. Cincor had changed. Zothique had changed. History had changed, had been denied.

Above in the blackness, tiny points of light, a myriad of stars, dotted the night, their feeble light glittering on the desolate plain where Maraeva had once been. Yet, in this new history, this new Cincor, this new Zothique, the barren plain had always been but a barren plain and nothing more. And in the whispered legends and tales of Zothique, there had never been a village called Maraeva.

Lest Darkness be Strength

It was night. A blood red moon dodged the sparse cloud cover, intermittent shafts of moonlight cascading down, tinting the dark landscape a dull red.

Three men rode on camels along the edge of a ridge topping off into a plateau. They were cloaked in black hooded riding robes, their hoods drawn up, concealing the soft red glow of their eyes. They were assassins of the Verilod. They rode for the cause of evil. A brotherhood of assassins in service to the King of Dloth.

The assassins reined their camels to a stop. They peered into the valley that extended from the ridge in a down sloped desolate and dusty land of rocks, crags, boulders, and cliffs. Mysterious shadows lurked there, shadows the moonlight couldn't penetrate. There were rumors about this land that extended southwest toward the legendary ruins of Chaon Gacca, former capitol of Tasuun. Great warriors had disappeared never to return; moans and cries of agony and anguish could be heard racing across the desolate landscape like the cold wind of death; and strange misshapen shadows were known to lurk near valley paths.

"Ahead is a path that leads beyond the valley," said Colus Jaar, glancing back with his one good eye at his Verilod companions. They had pulled up behind him. Jaar paused as he peered into the darkness beyond. He adjusted the patch that covered his shattered left eye. "I'm sure it's his course."

"Then it shall be our course as well," growled a companion.

"He goes not to the valley?" growled another.

Jaar grunted as he shifted in his saddle. "Would you?" he said, more a challenge.

The other remained silent, staring.

The assassins continued on their course, dodging shadows that crawled along the ridge. Soon the path would carry them across the face of the plateau to the edge of the valley. Beyond lay the desolate land that lead southwest to Chaon Gacca. Below, in the valley, cries echoed in the dark. The dark momentarily extended over the ridge to blend with the black horizon as the moon was swallowed by a cloud only to reappear minutes later as the cloud continued on its journey unabated across the sky.

"I've changed my mind," Jaar growled, his one good eye on the newly emerged blood moon. "We take the valley. Come." Nudging his camel, he turned toward a path that led into the black valley.

* * *

Kal Garec gazed at the top of the ridge. The moon reappeared from behind a cloud and bathed the ridge top in dull red light. Against the red-litten ridge were black shadowed forms of three Verilod. They were following the same path Garec had followed from the ridge to the edge of the valley. There was fear in his eyes, his normal eyes. Garec didn't possess the red glowing eyes as those who pursued him. They were Verilod. Garec was human. The Verilod weren't. He ran with a purpose; fear of death. His own.

A sudden cry of agony caused Garec to shift his gaze. There were sucking sounds in the nearby dark. A whispering gurgle and then silence. Only for a moment. Then something was dropped amidst the rock and dust that littered the valley floor. A body. And footsteps. Heavy footsteps. The footsteps were near, coming closer. *Which would be worse?* Garec thought. *The Verilod or the thing...* Garec's train of thought ebbed from approaching disaster to focus on death. He knew certain death lay with either prospect. And turning his eyes back to the ridge, he found the three shadows were gone. But they were out there, somewhere, in the dark. They were closer now, coming down from the ridge along the path that he had followed.

They would stop at nothing to punish him, to destroy him. Neerana was dead. Reja Vulsh was dead. Three Verilod assassins were now trailing him. Soon he'd be dead.

Garec hurried along the path in the dark, kicking stones out of the way, kicking up dust, tripping and sprawling to the ground in his haste. He forced himself to his feet and hurried on. He followed the path on its southwesterly course unknowingly headed toward Chaon Gacca. But the ancient Tasuunian capitol was miles away. At least a three day journey. There was no one there to afford Garec protection or sanctuary. Only the dead.

The path twisted and turned, meandering uphill and making Garec's effort more tiresome. His face and hands were stinging, cut and bloodied from rock and stone. He paused to catch his breath, his thoughts drifting to that day he had found Neerana dead. Images raced through his mind in tired segments. They were jumbled, out of sequence, but they were all there. He tried to correlate them, but fatigue from the uphill climb clouded his mind. Just the highlights he could see clearly. Over and over those horrible images flashed.

Neerana had started to town alone. It had been months since she had gone to town on her own. But the raids had stopped. Garec and Neerana had thought it safe - a tragic mistake. She hadn't come back by the time the bloated red sun had begun its descent in the western sky. Only the camel she'd been riding. It had returned riderless.

Garec had gone looking. He found her hanging between two wooden poles, her wrists bound by leather thongs. Four arrows protruded from her chest. They were black arrows with red fletching and three red rings around the shafts. A rolled piece of parchment had been shoved in her mouth. And the letter "V" had been carved into her forehead. Unmistakable. All of Dloth knew what it meant. The trademark signature of a Verilod killing.

Hesitant for fear the Verilod may still be near, Garec had glanced cautiously about before slowly approaching Neerana. He pulled the parchment from her mouth, unrolled it, and peered at the words.

She made good target for my arrows.

Garec had let her die. Nothing would bring her back. Something had to be done. A sudden hatred of everything Verilod had gripped his mind. He had stood peering down at Neerana's lifeless form. *There was time*, he had thought. *Yes, there was time.* He'd take her body home then he'd have revenge. *The Verilod will come to know their mistake.* He would make certain of it.

The images of the near past suddenly flashed from Garec's mind. Something had caught his attention. He paused on the path, glanced back then turned his eyes to the black form silhouetted against the night sky. It was uniform in shape, but with rough edges across the top. *A tower,* Garec thought. It was a crumbling tower, the bell tower of an ancient abbey. The path Garec followed was leading to it.

*   *   *

Jaar grumbled under his breath, moaning his disapproval of the path he and his companions were now traveling in their quest for Garec. The soft red glow of Jaar's one good eye flared. His hatred for Garec flashed through him, feeding energy to his glowing eye. The Verilod lived by hatred, innate evil, but this was different. It was personal.

There had been dissension of late among the Verilof leadership. Many had been positioning for power to vie for the title of Supreme Verilod. But the title came by choice. The decision of the Supreme Verilod himself. The Supreme Verilod was growing old. Reja Vulsh would choose a successor, and it was general knowledge that Vulsh favored Jaar. *But now,* Jaar thought, slowly shaking his head with anger and disgust, *but now this common human has destroyed that!* No one would know who Vulsh would've chosen.

Garec had destroyed the natural order of succession among the Verilod. Jaar found himself 'in-waiting' instead of being Supreme Verilod as was his want, his belief. With Vulsh's death an emergency council had been called. The six member council had voted for a new Supreme Verilod. The great asssassin, Maru Tralki, had been chosen. Only once before had the Supreme Verilod been chosen by a six member council. That had been over three centuries ago when Dloth was but a province of Tasuun and the Tasuunian kings had ruled from Chaon Gacca. Jaar knew that generations would pass before the same situation would again present itself, if ever. More so, Jaar and Tralki had been at odds. An intense dislike for one another. When Tralki would grow old and choose a successor, his choice would not be Jaar. By then Jaar himself would be too old to serve as Supreme Verilod. Garec had dashed Jaar's ambitions. Now the human had to pay. Jaar would delight in Garec's death. It would be a death painfully slow and agonizing.

Jaar drew his camel to a stop. His companions pulled up behind him. Jaar was impatient - the uphill effort on the path was tiring. But his madness drove him on, kept his mind reaching ahead into the darkness of the valley. Ahead somewhere in that black valley was Garec. Ahead somewhere in that black valley was death. And the thought of the human's death made Jaar smile. Yes, slow and agonizing it would be. *Perhaps peel his skin with my knife while he lives and make a coat. Leave his body to rot. Carrion for predators in this accursed valley.*

"Carrion," Jaar chuckled softly then burst out in wild maniacal laughter. He tilted his head back as he laughed then turned to his companions. "Death comes swift at the hands of the Verilod," he laughed. The laughter echoed through the darkness of the black valley as they continued down the path Garec had passed over a few scant minutes before.

* * *

In the dull light of the blood moon, Garec peered about. Across a flagstone courtyard rose the ruins of a great stone edifice. The ancient abbey. A ruined wall encircled the courtyard, ending at the path in a ruined gate. The collapsed ruins of the gate arch lay at the foot of the path where Garec stood. A great bell tower lay in ruins near the abbey's entrance, the weather rusted and pitted bell lying on its side, silent and unmoving. Recessed in the stone entrance of the abbey was a great oaken door, closed like a great eye oblivious to the cries of the destitute and dying in the black valley night.

Forms of black grotesqueness towered beyond the crumbling wall. Wind carved rock formations and the rising cliff face were etched in the inky blackness against the night sky with ghostly swirling dust devils caught by the red glow of the moon. The rock formations stood like great malformed beasts circling the abbey and waiting to claw whoever came forth. But no one did. No one had for nearly a generation.

Garec's eyes traced his faint shadow on the flagstone that was cast by the soft red light of the moon then turned and peered into the dark along the path that brought him to the ancient abbey. Somewhere back there were the Verilod assassins who were pursuing him. The path would bring them to the abbey as well. There was no other course, no other path. Garec was trapped. Despair gripped him. He turned his eyes to the shadow shrouded abbey entrance. Someone had to be there to afford him protection, to grant him sanctuary.

He hurried across the courtyard to the abbey entrance. The great oaken door was barred. A rusted lock hung on a ring from the door bolt. In desperation Garec shook the rusted lock, stepped back, and peered up the stone face of the abbey. Above, in the open arch of a small window, was the soft yellow glow of candle light. Someone was there. With a premonition of death, Garec turned back to the door and hammered with both fists.

"Help!" he screamed. "Help me!"

There was silence.

For many long moments there was silence as Garec pounded on the doors and begged sanctuary.

Then came a soft weary voice from inside. "Go away."

"Open the door!" Garec begged.

"Go away."

"They'll kill me if you don't let me in!"

"If they seek your death, then they must have cause," came the soft uncertain voice from behind the door.

"Verilod need no cause," Garec replied. "You must help me."

"You speak of the Verilod," came the voice. "The Verilod are evil. By its very nature, evil begets evil. So, by your nature, you must be evil as well."

"I only sought revenge for the death of my dear Neerana! One of them for her!"

"All that was good and just in these lands parted long ago. You shant find peace here."

Shocked into silence, Garec laid his head against the door, his hands splayed out above him. He closed his eyes and gritted his teeth. Soon it would end. The Verilod would have their revenge upon him. He would lie in a pool of blood at the foot of the abbey door. No one would know. No one would care.

How was he to know he had killed the Verilod leader? The Supreme Verilod didn't look any different than any of the others. It was the drums which had drawn Garec to them. And it had been convenient. A seemingly lone Verilod assassin on the hillside with a bow and quiver of arrows. Garec's act of vengeance had been done. Only then had Garec noticed another Verilod assassin standing near the crest of the hill watching. Garec had run, had been running ever since. For two days. Soon he would run no more.

There had to be a way out. He could not give up. *Perhaps the fallen stones...,* he thought as he peered about wildly. *Gain the top of the wall then into the valley beyond this place.* It was worth a try. A momentary pause as he glanced at the closed abbey door then he turned and skirted the stone wall to the left, looking for a low point in the ruined wall that he could scale and escape.

* * *

Inside the abbey the abbot stood with an ear against the great oaken door. Outside, the sound of running feet trailed away. Then there was silence. The man had gone. The abbot turned away and shuffled across the floor of the abbey's grand entrance and paused next to a wall mounted torch. The torch flame shown dimly in his sad and tired eyes. His heart was heavy. The stranger had wanted peace and security. But the abbot had turned him away just as the abbot had turned away from all that was just and good so many years ago.

Now there was nothing left but silence and loneliness in his small insecure world. His had been a soul corrupt. The abbot frowned as he reflected. Light and Dark. Law and Chaos. Good and Evil. Evil had won in the end. Corruption had settled over the land like a plague, stretching across the heart of Zothique from Zyra to Celotia. And desolation had crawled to the wall surrounding the abbey and its' courtyard. Dark things of sorcery began to roam the desolate lands. And creatures of loneliness like the old abbot. The abbot had become lord and master over desolation and death. The darkness that had settled over the land also festered in the old abbot. It had caused him to retreat within the walls of the decaying abbey. There he had grown old. The darkness bore down upon his soul. The abbey fell into rapid decay. He was alone. He had turned away from Dloth, from Zothique, and from humanity.

He had been wrong. He knew he had been wrong. Now there was a chance to redeem himself, an outside chance to help his fellow man. But he had turned his fellow man away to face the wrath of Verilod assassins. *Yet, is he not like them? Is he not as evil as they if he sought vengeance?* It didn't matter. The man outside in the courtyard was still his fellow man. The Verilod were not. The old abbot knew all things good and just wouldn't listen. But darkness would. Only in darkness could the old abbot redeem himself. *Evil begets evil* the abbot remembered telling the stranger. How befitting. *Evil does not distinguish between good and bad. Evil acts for its own gain, its own reward. Yes, evil begets evil.* The old abbot slowly nodded. *And evil will destroy evil.*

"All these years...," the old abbot muttered as he hung his head in despair and fell silent.

Tears came to his eyes. He had to do something. Soon his life would be at an end and there would be eternal unrest. There had to be one last act of good to surface from the darkness of his soul. The uncertainty he felt would end. Only then could he rest in peace. "Evil begets evil," the old abbot whispered as he turned his eyes to the blackness of the vaulted ceiling. He gave voice to his thoughts. "Evil will destroy evil. Let darkness be his strength."

"Please, you've got to let me in!" came Garec's pleading voice from the other side of the door. He was again pounding on the door with clinched fists. The ruined wall had been much too high to scale.

His thoughts interrupted, the old abbot slowly turned his eyes to the great abbey entrance and smiled. There was no need to open the door. The Verilod were not to be feared. The old abbot's smile widened. In the dark recesses of the entrance an unseen evil reared like a great shadow. The evil was formless, a black void surging toward the door. The torch in the entrance hall flickered and died. The hall was plunged into darkness. The abbot felt the last vestige of evil course from him as the black formless thing flowed against the abbey door.

"No need to worry, my friend," the old abbot whispered in a feeble voice as Garec continued to pound on the abbey door. "Your vengeance shall be returned a hundred-fold."

*　*　*

The sound of camel hoof beats echoed through the dark as the Verilod assassins approached the flagstone courtyard. Garec turned and stared wide-eyed. Jaar and his two companions dismounted just inside the gate on the opposite side of the courtyard. Jaar's one good eye was glowing bright as he stepped away from his camel. In the moon's soft red light Garec saw Jaar smiling. It was a smile of triumph. The Verilod assassin had won.

Garec turned and faced Jaar squarely. It was over. There was no escape. The high stone wall circled the courtyard, a wall Garec couldn't surmount. Across the courtyard the three Verilod assassins blocked the gate. And the door to the decaying abbey was locked and bolted. Garec glanced over his shoulder at the door, hoping the abbot had had a change of heart. The abbot hadn't. The door remained closed, a black mass set in the soft red moonlight that bathed the abbey walls. But there was something strange, something different, about the door. About the blackness.

The blackness was alive. The door seemed to pulse like a living organism. The blackness was absolute like the black shadows of the desolate valley. And there was a power that Garec didn't recognize, couldn't recognize. Time seemed to slow, to crawl. It seemed to take an eternity for Garec to turn and face Jaar again. When he did, he faced an arrow coming directly at him on a current of air.

Images suddenly flashed in Garec's mind. He saw Neerana, dead and impaled with black arrows. There was the glow of Jaar's eye across the courtyard; the darkness of the desolate valley and its lurking shadows; the falling body of the dying Supreme Verilod.

Still the arrow came. And Garec stood still. Not moving. Not afraid. A new feeling coursed through him, something different, something powerful. He felt change. His perception changed, emotional and spatial. He found himself looking down at the seemingly slow moving arrow. There was a crackling of bones and a tearing of garments. There was a fire in his head, and an intense flaring of hatred behind his eyes. Dimly, Garec saw Jaar stagger backward in horror, dropping his bow on the flagstone. Jaar's companions had already disappeared into the dark of the night. They wouldn't get far.

Then the arrow was there. Garec brought his huge transformed gnarled hand forward and picked the arrow out of the air. It shattered in his hand. He tossed it aside. It didn't hurt him as it had Neerana. But he didn't remember Neerana, nor the arrows which had pierced her heart, nor the letter "V" which had been carved into her forehead. Garec had forgotten. He didn't know where he was, why he had come to this desolate place, or why these sorcerous assassins had pursued him. But they had. In the deep recesses of Garec's churning mind, only one thought remained – the death of the Verilod.

Jaar scrambled for his camel. He took passing notice that his companions had already fled. It didn't matter. All that mattered was to get away from the thing. It had just plucked his arrow out of the air, crushed it, and tossed it aside like child's play. The thing wasn't a child. It wasn't Garec either. Jaar witnessed the change in the human, a change that happened in an instant. What had been a six foot tall man was now a twelve foot tall monster long of fang, claw, and horn. The thing rocked back and forth on its feet while some kind of lethal fluid dripped from its fangs and hissed as it pooled on the flagstone.

Before Jaar could mount his camel and flee, the thing lumbered across the courtyard and grabbed the Verilod assassin by the hood of his cloak. It raised Jaar to eye level, glared at the terrified assassin then shredded him with its great black talons in an explosion of blood and flesh. Jaar's screams still echoed through the black night of the desolate valley as the thing tossed the bloody mass of the Verilod assassin to the ground.

Into the dark night of the desolate valley the thing lumbered. Anything crossing its path would meet sudden death. The dark mysterious creatures of sorcery that dwelt in the valley cringed in fear of it, gave it ample leeway. The thing lumbered on with a terrible vengeance. Gone was any semblance of humanity. Gone was the knowledge of a dead companion. Only death raged in its' mind – death to be vented upon the Verilod. Why the Verilod the thing couldn't remember. Simply the Verilod. And before the night was out, there wouldn't be a Verilod assassin left alive in all of Dloth.

Silence descended upon the courtyard of the ancient abbey. The door swung slowly open. The old abbot stood in the door, peering across the flagstone courtyard at the bloody mass that had been Jaar, a Verilod assassin. *It's on its' way*, the old abbot thought. *Evil begets evil.*

"Vengeance returned a hundred-fold," the abbot whispered, adding after a pause, "Death shall come unto death this night."

He closed the abbey door on the outside world.

Glardun's Jewel

Jora Karrin glanced at the thick fog that clung to the ground. She swung her right foot and watched the tendrils of fog swirl about. The fog was unearthly, damp and musty. And it had an eerie shimmer. Karrin was convinced the fog was sorcerous.

"...getting thicker," she was saying, peering with uncertainty from behind the boulder where she and friend, Buraus Rhil, stood.

"What?" Rhil asked, a hand resting on his sword hilt.

"The fog. It's getting thicker."

"Sure as Thasaidon, I shouldn'ta let you talk me into this!" Rhil complained. "First we're run out of Zul-Bha-Sair. Then we're holed up in some ramshackle hovel of a place called Cith barely eking out an existence. Now you've got us looking for some jewel that may not even exist! You'll be having the Black Sorceries of Naat called down on us! I swear you're trying to get us killed."

Karrin chuckled. She shook her head. "Don't worry, my friend. The jewel exists. It's our ticket home to Zul-Bha-Sair. They'll be glad to see us back again."

"So you say," Rhil said softly as he peered cautiously about. "I'd like more proof."

Rhil reached up to stroke the dark brown fur of Ira, his pet *blavek*. The blavek sat perched atop the boulder. At Rhil's touch, Ira cooed, ruffling his great leathery wings. The blavek's two foot long body was supported by two great taloned feet. The curving talons extended six inches, dangerous and deadly to a blavek's prey. His leathery wings spanned seven feet. He sported two piercing black eyes. At the end of his long facial snout, two seven inch fangs curved from the roof of his mouth. Under Rhil's control the blavek was quite docile, but on command, the blavek would become a vicious, and quite efficient, killing machine.

"If Glardun's Jewel is made of the same gemstone as the Five Stars of Gavanti...," Karrin began. She fell silent. Ira had shifted his position and bared his fangs in a snarl.

The blavek's acute hearing had picked up a sound that Rhil and Karrin couldn't hear. Karrin shifted her feet and stared at the fog. *Something's out there. This is sorcery.* She moved her sword hand from the black leather bullwhip that hung from her sword belt to the jeweled hilt of her scimitar. Rhil, impatient for a fight, had already drawn his saber.

Suddenly there was a shadow. It lurched in a stiff gate as it moved toward the boulder where Karrin and Rhil stood. A definite shape took form as it appeared out of the fog. It was a man, or what had once been a man. Then there were more. They lurched forward, their decaying hands outstretched. There were gurgling sounds, groaning, and one of the walking dead howled like the wind of death.

Rhil was terrified. Karrin stepped from behind the boulder and raised her scimitar. For a moment the dead man closest to them stopped and glared. It reeked of death, empty eye sockets glowing orange, skin blue and peeling from a grinning skull. Tattered rags, soiled and blood stained, hung loosely from its decaying shoulders. Slowly it raised a gnarled hand and beckoned to the two adventurers from Zul-Bha-Sair. Bones protruded from the broken skin, two fingers missing. Others of its kind began to gather around it.

In revulsion Rhil stepped back. "I think I'd rather spend a night in the necropolis at Chaon Gacca," he growled softly.

"And miss all this fun?" Karrin laughed over her shoulder.

There was a sudden predatory cry from Ira. The blavek was still perched atop the boulder, a glare of hatred in its eyes. Great taloned claws grated on the rock, wings were partially spread as though at any moment the blavek would take to the air on a trail of death and destruction.

"Get it Ira!" Rhil suddenly blurted out.

The blavek was suddenly airborne and disappeared into the fog. It reappeared, swooped toward the ground, claws outstretched at the thing still reaching its beckoning and decayed hand toward Karrin and Rhil. Then the blavek was there. Great talons sunk deep into the dead man's head. There was a sickening snap as the skull cracked under the force of the blavek's claws. A putrid yellow puss-like slime erupted from the splintered head, showering the ground. The thing screamed in agony as though it were alive. The blue skin of its neck began to tear. With a snap of its neck, its headless body collapsed. The blavek disappeared back into the sky, the dead thing's shattered skull dangling from the talons.

"That's some pet you have there," Karrin grinned.

"Yes, isn't he though?" Rhil smiled as he joined Karrin.

"We're not finished yet," Karrin replied coolly, turning her gaze back to the walking dead a few yards away.

"I wonder just how many there are?" Rhil questioned softly.

"I don't know, but let's find out."

Karrin raised her scimitar, poised to strike. Rhil raised his saber. The walking dead, passive for now, huddled around the fallen body of their companion. Karrin watched, waiting for sudden movement. There were none. After a few moments, the walking dead began to back away. Then they were gone, back into the thick fog.

There had been many strange things in Karrin's life, but animated corpses? There had been stories of the Mykrasian Mountain passes. And stories she'd heard in her youth about the two sorcerers who'd come from Naat and raised the dead of long extinct Cincor. But those had just been stories. Now she knew there was truth to those old stories.

There had also been tales about zombies in the foggy mountain passes. And the name of a mysterious sorcerer called Glardun. It was said that the sorcerer lived in a cave in the Mykrasian Mountains. But no one ever saw. No one knew. Only the stories whispered at night behind closed doors.

That was Cincor and the Mykrasians. In Karrin's homeland of Zyra, magic and sorcery were also the norm, but to a lesser degree. Karrin knew of potions and spells. And the Swords of Light. Zyrans knew the old myths and legends. The greatest legend of all was the

Five Stars of Gavanti. Nobody had ever seen the Stars. Their very existence was in doubt. *But if it's true that Glardun's Jewel is made of the same gemstone as the mythical Stars...*

"It shall bare the proof," Karrin continued her aloud.

"Prove what?" Rhil asked.

"The Five Stars of Gavanti," Karrin replied. "If Glardun's Jewel is made of the same gemstone, then the Stars must exist."

"That doesn't prove anything, my friend," Rhil said. "We can't be sure. No one has ever seen the Stars. Even if we can get Glardun's Jewel, we still won't know if it's made of the same gemstone."

"They call it the Fire Stone," Karrin said. "There's supposed to be nothing like it in all the world. We shall see."

Karrin fell silent and watched the fog. The thick blanket had risen above them. It swirled in the sky, impairing their vision. A piercing cry echoed through the air and reverberated off the high stone walls of the fog shrouded mountain pass. A figured loomed ahead. It was another of the walking dead coming toward them. Two more loomed behind. They were regaining their courage, their determination to rid the mountain pass of these two living people.

"By Thasaidon, they just don't give up," Rhil said softly.

The zombie broke through the fog, its two companions close behind. It approached, armed with a saber. Karrin gazed at its dead face. The zombie was grinning. Its eyes were glowing more fiercely than had the eyes of its companion who met final death at the talons of the blavek. Karrin remained silent. She watched it approach; gauged its distance. *Close enough.*

In one quick motion Karrin brought a hand up, gripping the handle of her long black leather bullwhip. She balanced herself with the scimitar in her other hand. The bullwhip uncurled as it snaked in the air. In an instant the crack of the whip's tether echoed through the fog. The leather cord cut through the dead man's neck. Its head toppled from its body just as another stepped from the dense fog.

A cry echoed above. Karrin and Rhil looked up. In the fog a dark shape on great wings was looming. The blavek dove on one of the walking dead. In a flurry of flashing talons, the dead thing's headless body toppled to the ground. Ira disappeared back into the fog.

Still, there were more. And armed. They loomed in the fog, sabers raised, and lumbered toward Karrin and Rhil. Karrin dropped her bullwhip and met the first walking corpse as it swung its saber. Karrin countered with her scimitar. The force of the parry threw the dead man off balance. Karrin came around and cut the dead man in half at the waist.

"Where in the name of Vergama are they coming from?" Rhil shouted as more of them poured from the fog.

"I wish I knew!" Karrin shouted as a group of the walking dead began to surround them.

The walking dead circled the adventurers. The blavek suddenly appeared, rode a current of air to perch atop the large boulder, and cried a challenge to the walking dead. There was rage in the blavek's eyes, rage that mirrored impending destruction. A brief pause and the blavek was back in the air, hovering above the walking dead. Out of saber rage, Ira lunged, one by one, gouging with his great talons. The walking dead fell before the blavek's onslaught. Still, more lumbered out of the dense fog. The blavek couldn't stop them all.

"Back to back!" Karrin cried as the dead men closed the circle.

Rhil swung behind Karrin. The two turned in a circle. The ring of zombies was several ranks thick. They leered at the two adventurers; their orange eyes glowed brighter as they fed on the energy of an impending victory. A nearby zombie cackled with mad laughter. The laughter enraged Karrin. She swung out with her scimitar. The laughing dead man's saber was not there to counter the scimitar, and the zombie was severed at the waist. A wail of agony erupted as it crumpled to the ground. The rest raised their sabers. They stumbled over their fallen companion and closed on Karrin and Rhil at a slow shuffle. There was no way to take them all. Karrin resigned herself to her fate. But she'd take as many of them with her as she could. The knowledge brought her peace. And she smiled as the ring tightened.

Above, a sudden blue light shimmered through the fog. The walking dead saw and stopped their approach. They peered into the sky then turned and shuffled away, disappearing one by one into the fog. Karrin and Rhil exchanged puzzled glances. The blue light had saved them.

Sorcery, Karrin thought.

The light began to burn away the fog. When it had dissipated, a large ball of brilliant white light descended from the sky and settled to the ground.

The walking dead were gone, vanished with the fog. The blavek appeared in the sky, cooing softly, gliding a current of air to perch on Rhil's shoulder. The beast rustled his wings and then folded them.

The light faded. A young woman stood in its place. She turned to face the two adventurers. Fair skinned, eyes a deep blue, hair light and cascading in wavelets over her shoulders. She wore a gem high on her forehead. Her gown was white and shimmered in the light of the sun that now bathed the mountain pass.

"We owe you our lives," Karrin said.

"It's possible I may owe you my life," she replied, her voice soft.

"I...the fog...the dead...?" Rhil stammered.

"Gone," the young woman said. "I've removed them."

"Removed them," Rhil said. "How?"

"Sorcery," came the curt reply. "I'm Dezhura. Once the greatest sorceress in all Izdrel."

Karrin hooked her scimitar to her belt then turned to Dezhura. "I'm Jora Karrin." She cocked her head and gestured to Rhil. "This is my friend, Buraus Rhil. We're from Zul-Bha-Sair, but lately of Cith. You said owing us your life, what do you mean by that?"

"I know you've come for Glardun's Jewel, else you wouldn't be here in this mountain pass," Dezhura said. "I seek a gem in the sorcerer's cave. It belongs to me."

"Explain," Rhil said.

"I was once the greatest sorceress in all Izdrel," Dezhura began. "Then Glardun came from the Isle of Naat. His powers were great, greater than my own. He took from me the only thing I had which afforded me protection from him, a jeweled pendant on a golden chain."

"How is it you are free of him now?" Karrin asked.

"I'm not free of him," Dezhura replied. "He still holds power over me and can summon me whenever he wishes."

"We'll get your pendant for you," Rhil replied with a nod.

"I would be forever in your debt."

Karrin picked up her bullwhip, coiled the leather cord, and clasped it to her belt. She glanced at Rhil then turned her eyes to the high cliff wall. At the base of the wall was an opening. The entrance to Glardun's cave. He was there, and the Jewel, and Dezhura's pendant. There'd be no time to waste. The sooner they got what they came for, the sooner they could distance themselves from the sorcerer and his walking dead.

"Well?" Karrin questioned, staring at the cave entrance.

"We've come this far," Rhil replied. "Wouldn't be right just to turn around and go home."

The two of them started toward the cave entrance, the blavek still perched on Rhil's shoulder.

"Wait!" Dezhura suddenly called out.

The adventurers stopped and turned. Dezhura waved an arm in a circle. A small ball of blue light appeared, hovering a few feet off the ground. "A light to guide you," she said softly.

The ball of shimmering light led the adventurers to the cave entrance. They entered. The light glided through the air above them, its soft blue glow bathing the cave walls. The cave was dank and musty, smelling of death. The walls were damp and smooth except where broken by a patchwork of green moss. Progress was slow. Karrin and Rhil moved with caution, weapons drawn, ready for anything that would hinder their progress. Ahead there was a soft red glow. They were nearing the chamber of the great sorcerer, Glardun.

The passage emptied into a cavern of natural stone walls. The floor was flagstone. Stone partitions like castle walls crisscrossed the floor at odd angles. Centered in a wall was an open arched door leading to a second cavern beyond, presumably Glardun's chamber.

Weapons drawn, Karrin and Rhil stood in the arched doorway to the second chamber. The domed natural ceiling was cathedral. The walls ascended into darkness. All about this second chamber bodies lay scattered in various stages of decay and adorned in various grotesque positions. Apparent adventurers who had come to seek the fabled jewel.

The red glow emanated from the fabled jewel. It rested in a bracket atop a stone altar. Glardun's Jewel was as large as a fist, spherical, its face cut in segmented facets. Burning within was an orange flame, the same fire that burned within the fabled Five Stars of Gavanti.

But it wasn't the fabled jewel that had arrested Karrin's attention. It was a stone dais and throne that stood in the center of the chamber. A mummy adorned in tattered rags lay sprawled upon the throne.

"He's dead." Rhil was incredulous.

"I'm not so sure," Karrin replied, barely a whisper.

Scimitar ready, Karrin slowly approached the throne. The tattered rags that once clothed the silent, motionless form were decayed with age. The garments had once been of the finest silk laced with gold. Skin was dried, parched, and stretched tight over the skull. Eye sockets were empty. Cobwebs and shadows dwelt where eyes had once been. On a skeletal finger was a golden ring adorned with a large red gem. A crown of gold inlaid with pearl and studded with gems of many colors rested atop the skull. And around the neck hung a pendant suspended on a gold chain.

The scimitar held tight for self-assurance, Karrin cautiously mounted the stone dais. She ascended the steps, leaned forward, and lifted the jewel with the tip of her scimitar.

"Dezhura's?" Rhil questioned from the base of the dais.

Karrin sighed and shook her head. She had been troubled, unsure. But no longer. "No; not Dezhura's," she said softly, and pulled the scimitar away. The jewel dropped against the mummy's tattered garments sending up a curl of dust.

"What?" Rhil questioned. "What are you talking about?"

"A hunch," Karrin began, "First, those zombies in the fog turned away in fear from the blue light that Dezhura created. Second, Dezhura said she was Glardun's captive. If Glardun was that powerful, she'd never have left the cave. Third, this pendant...," Karrin paused, tapped the pendant with the tip of her scimitar then turned her eyes back to Rhil. "Why would Glardun be wearing this around his neck if it was her protection against him? And fourth, he doesn't look like he's much of a threat to anybody right now."

"Dezhura...she's...Glardun?" Rhil questioned softly.

"There is no Glardun," Karrin said softly.

"Your friend is right."

The voice came from the chamber entrance. Karrin and Rhil turned. Dezhura stood inside the arched doorway. She snickered, delighted at the rouse. So easy to trap two more unwary victims.

"I'm Glardun," she said, voice haunting and hollow. "Dezhura Glardun. From Naat." She laughed.

"Why the stories?" Rhil questioned.

"Why the lies?" Karrin immediately added.

"It's not important," Dezhura cackled madly. "What's important is that you're here; two more subjects for the king."

"I'm not subject to any king," Rhil said, raising his sword.

With a cry of warning, Ira lifted into the air and disappeared into the dark near the vaulted ceiling. Dezhura looked up. The blavek was descending. The sorceress smiled. She invaded the beast's mind, sending waves of seething hatred and rage directed at his master. The blavek turned and arced across the cavern, talons outstretched and aimed at Rhil's head. Rhil looked up just in time to see the curved weapons of death raining down upon him. The blavek arrived and sank its fangs and talons deep into Rhil's head while wrapping its great wings around his skull and shoulders. Blood spattered while the killing machine shredded flesh.

Suddenly there was an eruption of flesh, blood, and bone. Rhil dropped his sword and staggered to one side as the blavek beat its great wings and rose a few feet above the stricken adventurer. The head was gone while flesh, blood, and gore ran down his chest. He stepped lightly, staggering amidst the skull and brain fragments that now littered the cave floor while fingers frantically scrapped at the torn neck. Suddenly he toppled over and lay still. There was silence in the cave but for the beating of Ira's great wings.

Bones suddenly creaked; dust fluttered. The mummy sprawled across the throne struggled to its feet. Karrin half turned before she was caught in the clutches of the animated monster. The thing held her fast as Dezhura crossed the cavern to the base of the stone dias. The sorceress smiled as she raised a hand and waved her fingers. Karrin's scimitar melted from her grasp like water. Her bullwhip suddenly writhed snake-like from her waist belt.

"Goodbye," the sorceress said with a mad cackling laugh.

Suddenly, there were two quick snaps of the bullwhip. Karrin cried out as the tethers struck her eyes in rapid succession. Blood ran down her cheeks from empty eye sockets. The bullwhip snaked around her neck and synched tight, cutting off air. The mummu released its grip, and the bullwhip pulled Karrin high above the throne, lynching the adventurer. She kicked her feet, fighting feebly to free herself. But sorcery stretched the bullwhip taunt. Karrin couldn't free herself. Exhausted, her life fading, she became still and hung like an ornament above the throne.

Satisfied, Dezhura's laughter faded to a soft chuckle. She climbed the dias as the mummy in tattered rags slowly slipped down upon the throne. Her fingertips trickled lovingly on the parched skin that stretched across the skull's cheek.

"Two more subjects for you, my dear Zotulla," Dezhura said with a smile. She leaned forward and kissed the king's mummified lips that were pulled back and curled in a perpetual snarl of death.

The Snow Crystal

1

The three thieves glanced about the dim smoke filled tavern. Not many patrons were present. The truth be told - not many people were left in all of Zothique. Made stealing that much easier. Except in Zul-Bha-Sair. Life there was violent, even for thieves. Gondar Vloc, Orod Balo, and Teela Vant had fled after a botched attempt at a jewel said to have strange powers. Had they have been caught, they would have been skinned alive for the pleasure of Zul-Bha-Sair's ruling warlord. Things just weren't the same anymore. A thief just couldn't make a living in Zul-Bha-Sair.

With their skin still on their backs, the three thieves had fled south to the coast of barren and nearly dead Yoros. Balo had had an idea. Somewhere to the south, south of Zothique, rumor had it that the mythical Snow Crystal lay hidden in some island cave. Crossing the Indaskian Sea was a prospect that Vloc didn't particularly care for. He had a loathing for water, especially vast expanses of water.

We'll just put out the word and listen, Balo had said. *I'm sure somebody'll wag their tongue.*

Their journey to Yoros had taken them to a collection of mud huts at the mouth of the River Voum. The small no-name hamlet had been founded by a few lawless refugees from Zul-Bha-Sair and Darcor decades after the Silver Death had passed through Yoros and King Fulbra had sailed to the south seas. The collection of mud huts was the only place in the former Kingdom of Yoros that exhibited habitation. Except, of course, for a few lawless renegades that plied their trade in the desolate dark hinterlands of the former kingdom.

The thieves arrived in the nameless hovel, hung out in the tavern, put the word out and listened. They were chided, jeered, scorned. Most laughed, said there wasn't any such crystal, and went on about their business, ignoring the thieves. Some stared down Balo and Vloc while offering services to Teela Vant then laughed heartily as they turned away. The thieves exchanged glances and frowned. This wasn't going to be easy, even for a two-bit dusty hovel of a town.

Then there was the old man in a dark corner of the smoky tavern. He sat there, an eye peeled. Watching; waiting. He wasn't laughing. *Snow Crystal.* The words had caught his ear. He knew the fabled crystal. More importantly, he knew where it could be found. He was Z'jar Kali, an ancient sorcerer who had come from Naat nearly a century before, one of the last to come across the sea from the Island of Sorcerers.

Slinking through the dusty shadows, Kali approached the table where the thieves sat. "You seek the fabled Snow Crystal," he said softly, leaning forward, fingers entwined at the waist.

"Go away, old man," Balo grunted, brushing Kali off.

Kali ignored Balo's comment. He glanced over his right shoulder then his left. The tavern had returned to its raucous indifference. Satisfied that no one was listening, Kali turned his attention back to the thieves. "It's a dangerous thing you seek, but...," Kali began.

"Old man...," Balo interrupted, his tone darker, threatening.

"Wait," Vloc said and patted Balo on the shoulder. He turned his eyes to Kali, and added, "Let the old man speak."

The old sorcerer paused, again looked over both shoulders, and when he turned his attention back to the thieves, his eyes were wide with excitement. "I know where it can be found," he continued.

Balo reached up, grabbed the old sorcerer by his cloak, and pulled him down into a chair at the table. "Tell us what you know," Balo growled, fingers still clutching Kali's cloak.

"Not here," Vloc suddenly said. Turning to Kali, he added, "Is there a place we can be alone?"

"My abode," Kali said softly with a smile. "I can show you..."

"Alright alright," Balo interrupted. "Too many ears to hear."

Kali's smile widened. "Then come," he said.

One by one, the three thieves followed the old sorcerer from Naat out of the tavern.

2

Z'jar Kali's abode was a small dusty single room hut, though well constructed and sturdy. More so than any of the other decaying huts in the hastily patched together hovel. A cot, book case, table, and chair were the only items of furniture in the hut. Strange exotic items and implements beyond the knowledge of the thieves littered the single room. Stacks of books teetered on the edge of the table, on bookcase shelves, and in corners of the room.

"*A History of Toskian Pirates,*" Vant casually read a book cover. She moved on to the next, lifting the cover slightly. "*Raising the Dead,*" she read, let the cover drop, and turned to Kali. "Have you raised the dead?"

"I have read about it," he replied with a slight grin. "The dead do not like to be raised. You have to offer them something in return." His grin widened as he nodded to the book. "At least that's what it says in that book."

"So, what are you, old man, some sort of wizard?" Vloc said as he fingered a strange glass container on the table. There was a green bubbling liquid in the container, a wisp of white vapor trailing off into the room.

"Just a collector," Kali said through a lopsided smile.

"You collect strange things," Balo added.

"Interesting things," the old sorcerer replied. "But it is not my meager trinkets and books that interest you."

"No, it isn't," Balo growled. He turned and stared the diminutive old man down. "You know where the Snow Crystal is."

"It lies to the south...," Kali began.

"To the south," Vloc interrupted, fearful of water. "Water." It was a muttered thought.

"The Indaskian Sea lies south," Kali said softly. "And islands. That's where the Snow Crystal lies. In a cave on a small island."

"There are dozens of islands between Yoros and Cyntrom," Vant said. "And even if we knew which island, how would we get there?"

"Go to the mouth of the Voum," Kali said. "There you will find a single sail skiff. Once to sea, the shadow currents will take you to the island. And bring you back."

"Shadow currents," Vant said, a statement rather than a question.

"The wind comes, the wind goes," Kali replied with a shrug of his shoulders. "The shadow currents will always be there." Without awaiting a reply, the old sorcerer turned to the table, picked up a small wooden box adorned in strange glyphs, and turned to face the thieves again. "You will need this."

Vant took the box the old man offered, inspected the strange glyphs that adorned it then opened the lid. A square piece of dried and treated human skin lay within. The skin was soft, like a yearling *taunga* hide. And it was adorned with the same strange glyphs that decorated the exterior of the box.

"What are these symbols?" she questioned as Balo and Vloc joined her for a closer look.

"I don't know what they mean," Kali said with a smile. "But they will protect you against the power of the crystal. It must be covered, else its power will plunge the land into perpetual winter."

"One of your books tell you that?" Vant questioned.

Kali nodded. "Yes, one of my books," he said smiling.

Balo wedged himself between Vant and Kali. Eyes narrowed, lips twisted in a sneer, he curled his fingers around the fabric of the old man's collar, and leaned close. "Don't tell anyone, old man," he growled. "Or we'll come back here and skin you alive."

There was a moment's pause, their eyes locked then Balo patted the old man on the shoulder and stepped back. He and his two thieving companions turned toward the door.

"No one has ever come back," the old man said softly, nodding to the box. "Those that have gone after the crystal. None have returned to tell their story."

The door opened, the thieves paused. Vloc was apprehensive, unnerved by the old man's words and the Indaskian Sea. Vant turned her eyes to Balo for a reaction. Balo stared at the old man. He was cold, indifferent.

"We'll be back," Balo suddenly said, and with his eyes still on the old man, he added, "Let's go."

The three thieves left the old man's shack. They didn't hear him chuckling after the door was closed.

* * *

The bloated red sun had long since set. The sky was black. A red wind blown dust swirled in the night air. Dim ancient stars darted amidst the dust clouds.

The thieves hurried from Kali's home, skirted a back alley, and made their way out of the decaying hovel. It didn't take them long. There wasn't much of a hovel to sneak out of. They made their way to the Voum River and followed its course to the south shore. It was a short distance and in no time they were there.

The skiff was there as well, just as the old man had said it would. It was small – a centerboard single sail vessel with three bench seats and four oars for rowing if the need arose. *Strange,* Balo thought, *like it was made for us.* For Vloc, it was small, dreadfully small. And as he lifted his eyes to the water of the Indaskian Sea, black under the veil of night, the skiff seemed even smaller.

"We're not getting anywhere just standing here," Vant said, and stepped into the skiff. There was a lantern lying on the center bench seat. She lit it, hung it on a hook protruding from the mast, and turned to the two men still standing on the shore. "Coming?"

The two men stepped into the skiff. An unnatural wind suddenly whistled through the dual line shrouds that supported the single mast. The sail quickly swelled and the skiff lurched forward. Balo and Vloc were thrown off their feet; they scrambled for a bench seat as the skiff headed out to sea under the cover of night.

3

By dawn the shores of Yoros had long since slipped from sight. Somewhere beyond the southern horizon several small islands were thrust up from the sea floor. And further still rose the large island of Cyntrom. But the thieves wouldn't reach the shores of Cyntrom. The island they sought, the Island of the Snow Crystal, lay somewhere between the shores of Yoros and Cyntrom.

Vloc was apprehensive. *A three day journey,* the old man had said. It might just as well be forever for Vloc. He muttered angrily under his breath. He hated the sea. It was the same everywhere. Never changing. Monotonous. And calm this day, eerily calm. And prone to create hallucinations or visions. Vloc stared at the single sail of their small craft. The wind had diminished. The sail hung limp against the mast. The sea was smooth like glass. A deathly silence had settled all around.

"Where's the wind?" Vloc said fearfully. "This is sorcery!"

"Don't worry," Vant said with a chuckle. "The wind comes, the wind goes. Like the old man said."

Vant's words did little to settle Vloc's nerves. He stepped back and slowly settled to the bench seat behind the mast.

"Look at this," Balo called out. Vant and Vloc hurried to port and peered into the water. There were figures beneath the surface. Forms, elongated shadows. They were swimming near the skiff. And they were everywhere.

"Shadow currents?" Vloc questioned.

Vant nodded. "Shadow currents," she said softly.

The skiff lurched forward. The sail fluttered against the mast. The shadow currents carried the skiff and its passengers south. All through the day the shadow currents were there. Then as the bloated red sun slowly slipped beneath the horizon, the shadow currents dispersed and swam away. The skiff rested motionless on the sea. The thieves sat there, silent, exchanging glances, and looking out across the water. The red dusk gave way to the black night. And one by one, the few ancient stars shown dimly in the sky above.

"Well?" Vloc questions apprehensively.

"Well what?" Balo growled.

"Where did they go?" Vloc replied. His voice was edgy. "Do we just sit here and wait for them to come back?"

"Gondar...," Vant began.

A sudden gust of unnatural night wind caught and filled their sail.

"I suggest we get some rest," Balo said as he stretched out as best he could in the bottom of the skiff.

The skiff glided on the water as the thieves slept. Beneath the surface of the Indaskian Sea strange lights appeared in many colors, some steady, some flashing. They followed the skiff through the night until the first red light of dawn then they were gone.

The wind carried the skiff south until the late afternoon of the second day. Then again, the wind died out, the sail hung limp, and the shadow currents appeared in the water. They took hold of the skiff and continued the journey south, further from Yoros, further from Zothique, closer to the mysterious island where the fabled Snow Crystal lay hidden in a cave. As the night settled in, the shadow currents swam away. The night wind and strange lights beneath the water reappeared, and as the three thieves slept through the second night, their journey continued.

The sun had risen blood red and bloated on the third day. A slight sea wind filled the sail, but the shadow current had remained to guide the skiff to its destination. This was the day, the third day. The old man had said that it would be a three day journey to the Island of the Snow Crystal. Some time today, Balo knew, they'd reach their destination and the Snow Crystal would be theirs.

"We should get rid of Vloc," Balo whispered to Vant. They sat together on the stern bench seat of the skiff as the afternoon sun was climbing down from the sky.

"What do you mean get rid of him?" Vant questioned softly.

"I mean kill him," Balo whispered his reply. "His whining irritates..."

"An island!" Vloc shouted from the prow where he'd been standing all day just waiting for the island to appear. He couldn't wait to get his feet on solid ground again.

Balo and Vant jumped to their feet and raced to join him. Sure enough, in the distance was an island on the horizon. And the shadow currents were barring them straight for it.

Before long the shadow currents veered off and swam away. The sea wind was enough to bring them ashore. It wouldn't be long. Vloc stared at the growing island shoreline and smiled. Balo glanced a side eye at Vant and smiled. But it wasn't the shore he was thinking about, nor the fabled Snow Crystal. It was murder. Vloc's murder.

4

The skiff had brought them ashore on a black rocky beach. They had run aground. The thieves jumped into the knee-high water and dragged the skiff onto the beach. Stretching arms and legs, they peered about. A cave entrance immediately caught their eye. It was layered in ice and snow, and the sound of a raging winter storm roared from within.

"That's it! THAT'S IT!" Balo shouted, laughed, and cried while he grabbed Vant and swung her around.

The thieves celebrated, dancing madly about. Then Balo grabbed Kali's ornately decorated box and they hurried across the beach to the cave entrance. A cold wind rushed from the cave and the three thieves shivered. They hadn't considered the cold inside the cave in their rush to acquire the Snow Crystal. But they had come too far to turn back. Their only hope and wish was that they didn't have to go too far into the cave to retrieve the fable Snow Crystal.

"Let's go," Balo said and entered the frigid cave.

Vant and Vloc followed close behind. The trio found themselves in a raging blizzard. Ice and snow were everywhere, the floor of the cave coated and slick. The cold wind howled in their ears and they squinted into the roaring snow and ice crystals. Body temperature began to drop. The blowing ice crystals stung. They fought the storm as they made their way deeper into the cave, every step taken a grueling fight forward. Their skin, hair, and garments glazed over in a thin film of frost. And they shivered uncontrollably in the rapidly worsening cold.

With Kali's box clutched tight against his chest, Balo fought against the wind, ice, and snow. He moved slowly, his body barely blocking the storm for the other two that followed close behind. Then Vloc gave in to the storm and slumped to the cave floor. Balo and Vant left him behind. They struggled on through the raging subterranean storm until Vant, too, slumped to the cave floor.

"Go on...get it and let's get out of here!" she insisted as Balo hesitated.

He paused, then nodded and went on alone. Slowly he made his way forward, deeper into the cave where it was eerily growing lighter. It was the light of the Snow Crystal, Balo was certain. He was right. The cave passage emptied into a hollowed out cavern. The wall and floor were thick in snow and ice. The wind howled as snow and ice crystals spun in a vortex about a short pedestal in the center of the cavern. A white light radiated from the top of the pedestal.

The Snow Crystal, Balo thought. He shielded his eyes and fought his way to the pedestal. There it was, smaller than a small man's fist, but powerful enough to plunge the world into perpetual winter.

Balo opened the box, took out the dried skin, and wrapped the crystal in it. The blizzard stopped; the raging winter wind stopped; the ice and snow began a slow melt. Balo placed the wrapped crystal in the box and closed the lid. Clutching the box to his chest, he breathed a sigh of relief. And then turned back the way he had come.

* * *

A day gone from the Island of the Snow Crystal, the shadow currents were carrying the skiff and its passengers north toward Yoros. Vant stared at the box that contained the fabled crystal. It was coated in a thin film of frost, the strange glyphs obscured. Balo stood leaning against the single centerboard mast, his eyes on Vloc, his mind plotting, planning. Vloc stood in the prow, eyes on the far northern horizon, longing for Zothique. He was smiling.

Hatred and contempt deepened. Balo's eyes and mood grew darker. Deadly. He stepped forward and reached for Vloc.

Pushed, Vloc went head first into the Indaskian Sea. The shadow currents scattered, setting the skiff adrift. Balo and Vant waited, watching the ripples fan out. Then Vloc surfaced, arms flailing, eyes wide with terror, begging for help.

"You're a dead man!" Balo shouted then roared with laughter.

Vloc's eyes widened. He gasped. But it wasn't Balo's words that terrified him now. Something had tugged at him. From below, from the sea. Again, a quick tug then a tentacle wrapped around Vloc's leg and dragged him under.

"Something got him," Vant said softly as the two thieves stared at the surface of the Indaskian Sea where Vloc had been.

A sudden rush of water erupted from the sea, showering the skiff. A tentacled monster suddenly rose from the depths, its tentacles writhing wildly about. In its grasp was Vloc, a tentacle wrapped around his legs, arms, and neck. A screeching howl rented the air. The tentacles pulled, and Vloc was dismembered and decapitated.

Vloc's severed head splashed in the water as the rest of his remains and the tentacled monster slipped beneath the waves. The head plopped into the skiff, bounced between two bench seats, and came to rest near Balo. Vant had stepped back to avoid the bouncing head. Balo picked it up by the hair and turned to throw it overboard. The eyes suddenly opened and the severed head of Vloc grinned.

"By the fires of Mordiggian," Balo whispered. He stared wide-eyed at the head for a moment then tossed it overboard. Vant slowly joined him and together they stared into the water.

Vloc's severed head bobbed on the surface while slowly turning to face the skiff. A tip of a tentacle suddenly curled over the top of the head. The eyes were staring up at Vant and Balo for a final time before the tentacle dragged it beneath the waves.

"That thing...it'll kill us," Vant squeaked, barely audible.

Balo glared at her then turned away without a word. He stomped around the skiff, muttering angrily to himself, slapped the mast with a clinched fist before finally sitting down on the center bench seat and staring at the frost covered box.

Vant stared at the surface of the Indaskian Sea. The tentacled monster hadn't return. Neither had the shadow currents. And no mysterious sea wind. The skiff drifted on the water. Balo and Vant waited. Still no sign of the tentacled monster or the shadow currents.

"We're stuck here...," Vant began to complain.

"The shadow currents will be back," Balo interrupted angrily.

The bloated red sun was slowly sinking in the western sky.

5

Far to the north black clouds were forming on the horizon. *A storm,* Balo thought. The low clouds churned south over the Indaskian Sea. Thunder roared. Lightning flashed. The sea began to swell. It was a sorcerous storm that was bearing down upon Balo and Vant from the north. From Yoros. And it was bringing the dark of night with it.

"Looks like it's going to get a little rough," Balo said. His eyes were on the gathering clouds as the sky began to darken.

Suddenly, a short distance away, there was movement just below the surface of the sea.

"See? The shadow currents," Balo said, pointing. "I told you they'd be back."

But there weren't any shadow currents. The Indaskian Sea began to bubble and churn. Hissing jets of water shot into the sky. Then the bow of a large ship broke the surface from beneath the waves.

Balo stumbled backward, almost fell, but was caught by Vant.

"What in the name of Mordiggian...?" Vant's voice trailed off as the ghost ship rose from the water.

In minutes the ghost ship rested on the surface of the Indaskian Sea. Waters lashed against its rotting hull. Seaweed hung tangled in its rigging and from its yards. Sails hung limp, torn, and charred. The mizzen and upper mainmast were gone. Bloated dead bodies in various stages of decay hung by their feet from yards and lines. There was evidence of destruction – shattered wood, charred hand rails and bulkheads. The ship was thick with slime and barnacles.

The apparition turned slowly in the churning waters and glided toward the small skiff. The oncoming night and black clouds shrouded the ghost ship while flashes of lightning highlighted the oncoming horror. Expectant shouts echoed through the raging storm. As the ghost ship neared, Balo and Vant saw the main deck rail was lined with worm eaten Toskian pirates waving rusted sabers. They were brutish and bestial things in death as in life; apish animals violent and deadly with no compassion.

On the quarter deck stood a lone figure. A tall brutish man – dead, pale, worm eaten, tattered long coat, his clothing soaked through with seaweed draped over his shoulders. This was the pirate captain. As Vant looked up at him, his glowing eyes met hers. His smile widened. A chill of death ran through her.

Grapping hooks swung out of the night. Vant and Balo dodged them, tripped over the bench seats, and sprawled into the bottom of the skiff. The dead pirates howled and cackled as they hauled on the lines with uncanny strength. Little by little the skiff was inched up the side of the ghost ship until it reached the main deck hand rail. Decaying hands grasp the skiff and dragged it over the hand rail and onto the main deck. Vant and Balo looked up into a ring of grinning pale worm eaten cackling dead faces that surrounded them.

"Move aside!" a voice bellowed. "Move aside ye dead swine!"

The swarm of dead pirates parted as the captain approached. There was a brief pause as the dead captain's eye lingered on Vant then he reached for both and dragged them out of the skiff.

The pirates split as one group swarmed around Balo and the other swarmed around Vant. The two were separated, pulled apart, Balo toward the mainmast while Vant was dragged toward a grated hatch cover on the aft main deck.

Suddenly they stopped and the raging storm that had descended upon them faded. The lightning was gone. The thunder was gone. The dead pirates hushed. All that was heard was a soft moaning of wind through the shrouds. Balo and Vant peered about wildly then turned their eyes in the same direction that the dead pirates were staring. Out of the sorcerous clouds a figure descended to the aft quarter deck and stood at the hand rail, looking down upon the charnel gathering upon the main deck. Balo and Vant recognized the small figure. It was the little old man who had directed them to the Snow Crystal. Z'jar Kali.

"I have delivered more victims for your pleasure," Kali shouted from the quarter deck. He raised a hand and pointed to the skiff. "The crystal."

The dead captain reached into the skiff and took the glyphed box from beneath the bench seat where Balo had placed it. He turned and looked up at Kali. "You have kept your end of the bargain," the dead pirate captain growled. "I shall keep mine."

The box lid swung open and the protective glyph covered human skin was pulled back to expose the crystal. Winter exploded, engulfing the ghost ship in raging wind, snow, and ice. The dead captain tossed the box and skin to the Naat sorcerer then turned to his crew and held up the Snow Crystal.

Kali was gone with his wooden box and dried human skin. The dead pirates howled in celebration. The old sorcerer from Naat had delivered two more victims to them. One would be murdered and strung up; the other would join them – after some enjoyable persuasion by the dead crew. They swarmed around the two new victims as the winter storm raged about the ghost ship. Waves broke across the decks. The ship was unmoved, riding steady on the surface. In no time the decks, bulwarks, masts, and yards were coated in ice; large icicles hung in the dark, glinting in the flash of winter lightning as the winter storm raged on. Snow swirled amidst the tattered sails and rigging. And lines snapped in the roaring wind.

Laughing and taunting, a group of dead worm eaten pirates cut off Balo's head as he begged for his life. They strung him up by his feet then hauled on the line. Balo's headless body swung from the mainsail yard while blood from his severed neck pooled on the icy deck. His head rolled across the main deck. It was the last thing Vant saw before she was dragged below deck by the dead pirates through the now opened hatch, pawing at her hair, clothing, and body.

The dead captain grinned as he watched the woman disappear below. The crew would have their fun with her, alive and dead, until she joined them.

The deck began a slow tilt. It was time to return to the sea. The ship's hull groaned then lurched violently. A great wave crashed across the deck, poured through the open hatch, and into the bowels of the ghost ship where several pirates had taken Vant.

The ghost ship was sinking once again. Slowly she settled into the sea. The hull and decks disappeared beneath the waves. Then the masts, yards, shrouds, tattered sails, and lines. The surface swam in a spiral then began to settle. In minutes the sea was calm. The storm passed on. Ancient stars shown in the night sky. Mirrored beneath the waves was the soft white light of the Snow Crystal that dimmed as the ship sank further and further toward the bottom of the Indaskian Sea.

* * *

A black cloud formed over the small island. Thunder rumbled from within as lightning cut across the sky. A film of thin ice quickly formed on the surface of the sea on the north side of the island. The ice sheet fractured, spider cracks shooting off in all directions, as six people broke through while walking from the sea floor toward the island. They were the dead Toskian pirate captain, four of his bestial crew, and their newest crewmember – the dead female who'd come looking for the Snow Crystal.

As they broke the surface, a raging winter storm generated by the Snow Crystal exploded upon the island. Each step brought the worm eaten dead pirates closer to shore, closer to the cave from whence the crystal had been taken. They were returning the crystal to its resting place upon the pedestal. And it would rest there until the next thieving adventurer would attempt to steal it – sent there by Z'jar Kali, the Sorcerer from Naat, as long as there were victims left to send. *Protect the crystal,* Kali had wanted of the dead pirates. And as Kali knew, the dead always demanded something in return.

A Moment Out of Time

1

"She's an old friend, Corod." Zan Travaale smiled. "A very old friend."

Travaale suddenly knew that he'd seen and said this all before. He'd already been here in the ruined garden of the Zharanet Estate on the outskirts of Oroth, speaking these same words. It unnerved him as he remembered. The ruins, the mysterious Ceara. *A moment out of time,* she'd said. He knew he'd live it again and again. Corod Valdhari and the others wouldn't. They didn't know. They wouldn't know. His smile widened as he turned his eyes to Valdhari. There was a distance in those eyes.

Valdhari studied Travaale, noted the look on his face, the deep distance in his eyes. Valdhari knew not to intrude on Travaale's inner thoughts nor press him further about the woman. If the Izdrel wanderer wanted to speak his thoughts, he would. It'd been years since they'd seen one another so as Valdhari remembered. Still, there was nothing he could say to entice his old friend to stay. Even for a short while. Travaale had always been a wanderer, always would be.

"Well, old friend, I do think it's time for me to go," Travaale said with a whispered nod. He turned away, looking north through the gnarled shrub to the parched landscape beyond.

Valdhari momentarily glanced in the same direction then turned his eyes back to the wanderer. "Where do you go now?" Valdhari questioned, knowing Travaale himself didn't know.

Travaale glanced at his old friend, paused in thought then spoke. "I'm not sure, perhaps Avandas or Aramoam," he said. "Someplace where I can get lost, blend in with the crowd." There was a pause then Travaale continued, "Time that I found a new life for myself."

Travaale knew better. He laid his saber across his right shoulder as Valdhari stepped forward and rested a hand on his left shoulder.

"Should you ever have cause to stopped wandering, you know you're welcome here," Valdhari said, forcing a smile.

Travaale remained expressionless. He'd be back, but not in the manner that Valdhari implied. There was a slight smile then Travaale responded with a nod.

"Fare well," Valdhari said.

The wanderer nodded and turned away. Valdhari watched as his friend left the ruined garden and disappeared down the rubble strewn street. Travaale was going north, moving on to a new life, forever the vagabond wanderer, forever wandering the desolate lands of Zothique in these latter days.

"I hope you find what you're looking for, old friend," Valdhari whispered his thoughts aloud after Travaale was gone.

* * *

Travaale wandered on foot along the Asparias River then turned north through the barren rusty desert of Celotia. To the east the ragged mountains that bordered Tasuun clawed at the sky. Travaale had decided on Avandas as his destination. Although the population was declining, it was a large enough city to blend in easily and not be noticed. In these dark times Avandas reminded him of Zul-Bha-Sair and Darcor, both lawless cities where people didn't question or ask names. It was enough to stay alive. No one bothered to know who had died. Or who may have been responsible. Travaale smiled. *Avandas, refreshing, that's where I belong.* His smile became a chuckle as he crested a rise. The rusty red desert of Celotia stretched before him. It wasn't long before the bloated red sun of Zothique's sky began its descent toward the horizon.

That first night was restless and cold. Travaale huddled in the dark, shivering, his hands tightly gripping the hilt of his saber. He had a fearful uneasy feeling. Maybe it was the strange cries coming from the dark. Maybe it was the strange feeling that had come over him like a thousand tiny needles pricking his skin. Maybe it was that he could've sworn something important was going to happen or had already happened and he couldn't remember. He shrugged, shivered, and his eyes darted in the night as a howling cry echoed out of the dark. Whether human, animal, or otherwise, he couldn't tell. But the sound faded and all grew quiet. Still, sleep wouldn't come.

The night wore on. Travaale found himself staring into the dark, his mind empty. The stars marched across the sky. Time passed. He sighed, listened, watched. He wondered at the thought of something happening...*had happened,* his mind corrected. *Or will happen.* He shook his head, frustrated by his sudden forgetfulness. It was puzzling. He felt no one invading his thoughts, no sorcery.

The stars, he thought and turned his eyes to the canopy above.

The stars twinkled in the black night. He studied them, watched their light, and wondered. There had been stories about the stars since time immemorial. Some said they were the souls of the dead; some said they were a reflection of the legendary Snow Crystal that could bring perpetual winter to the world; some said that they were great furnaces of fire, and some said that in olden times humans from his own world had traveled to the stars and had never returned.

Travaale chuckled. Star travelers, huge furnaces, souls of the dead. It made no matter. They were too distant, too constant, beyond reach to be of any concern; the abode of the gods. *But...the Snow Crystal.* Travaale shivered, and shrugged away the thought. That was something he didn't want to think about. A frozen world. His world. Sterile. Dead. An anonymous life in wild Avandas is what he sought. His thoughts were jumbled, filled with nightmare images, fleeting glimpses of stone ruins, and a mysterious woman. Finally, in the night, Travaale drifted off to sleep. And the stars continued their march across the sky until the rising of Zothique's bloated red sun.

2

The forest was dark, the land green. This was not barren Celotia. Nor was this craggy and desolate Tasuun. The jagged mountains to the east were gone. The sky was blue; the burning sun yellow and small, not the bloated red sun slowly crossing the orange skies of Zothique that Travaale knew. There was sorcery at work here.

By midmorning Travaale had traveled leagues through the strange dark forest. He moved slow, apprehensive, glancing about with uncertainty. The forest was dense, foreboding, steeped in shadow, and getting darker. The forest seemed sentient with a life of its own, watching through a myriad of unseen eyes. Cautiously, Travaale continued deeper into the forest. He followed a narrow twisting trail. The uncertain forboding feeling remained, something watching from the shadows. Instinctively, his saber was poised to strike. He tried to focus his thoughts, and keep his mind and eyes as keenly aware as possible. Who knew what manner of beasts lurked in the shadows, behind a tree, or underneath a clump of brush. Strange beasts plied such legendary forests of old – dark misshapen creatures that many said were once men who had turned their backs on the gods. *Such tales!* Yet, Travaale sensed some truth in them.

There was a rustling of leaves. Travaale stopped. The rustling softened then stopped as well. Whatever it was it had grown silent, perhaps trailing Travaale, waiting for a moment to strike. Travaale slowly raised his saber, ready to use it if necessary. And waited, watched. The sound didn't return. He continued on the path, peering about, watching for movement in the shadows. There were none, just the shadows themselves shifting as he walked. Deep in the forest the cries of strange beasts began to die away. Silence descended. The unearthly silence suddenly gave Travaale cause for concern. Not even in the desolate wastes of Tasuun was there such silence.

Travaale caught his breath. A soft sound intruded. It was a trickling sound; flowing water. Travaale followed the sound. As he neared, it became a rush of water. A torrential cascading of white water over rocks. It was a narrow and swiftly moving river. The water flowed past, the sun sparkling diamonds dancing on its surface, and small eddies of white foam slipping across river cobble. Travaale knelt at the water's edge and peered at his reflection. He studied the face – the piercing eyes, the square jaw, the long white hair. His mind momentarily went blank. Then his thoughts wandered far from the river. To the stone ruins and the mysterious woman.

Travaale shook his head and stood up. "She has something to do with this," he muttered, his eyes still distant.

* * *

Far off on a hillside the ruins of a castle round tower rose amidst a cluster of trees. *North,* Travaale surmised by the path of the small yellow sun across the sky. He had followed the course of the River Usk against its current until he had come to a branch, a tributary that wove into the hills toward the ruins. Here, with the sun riding high, Travaale had rested; here he had first absently espied the tower in the distance. *Someone has to be there,* he thought, hoping for answers. And north he turned, following the Rhiangoll toward the round tower amidst the trees.

The trees rose into the sky, cutting off the sun and casting a pall across the forest floor with long shades and mist. Things lurked in the shadows that Travaale had never seen, things he didn't want to see now. Dark shadowy things fluttered between branches high above, just out of the range of eye sight. There was a cacophony of noise from all around. Far ahead, deep into this new and wondrous land, if not foreboding and uncertain, Travaale thought he saw glimpses of more stone masonry.

Travaale drew his saber and paused, a cautionary action. He caught his breath short, his heart raced, and he waited before moving on. Nothing happened. Eyes and ears alert, Travaale continued on. The forest darkened as the day wore on, the sun slowly sinking toward an unseen horizon. Travaale suddenly stopped in the middle of a narrow path. Above, amidst the trees, was the soft fluttering of leathery wings. A small orange and red beast was perched on a tree limb. It looked down at Travaale and cooed softly. In the dim light he saw the small creature drop to the forest path. It sat there rocking gently on its hind feet, wings fluttering as it stared up at Travaale. The little beast glowed faintly, and Travaale noted a scent of burning sulphur. The little beast cocked its head and seemed to grin. And then belched. A plum of black soot erupted from its nostrils, curled in the air then faded.

"Who are you, my little soot snorting friend?" he questioned.

"His name is Spite," came a soft female voice from the dark.

Travaale looked up as a tall mysterious woman stepped from the shadows, the same mysterious woman that'd plagued his thoughts of late. She wore a shoulder strapped, light blue filmy gown. She was pale, looking of death, her long raven black hair falling in soft waves about her shoulders. Eyes piercing, her thin lips turned to a wry smile. And in those eyes Travaale saw a light of mystery.

She stepped forward, her smile untouched as she spoke. "I'm Ceara," she said softly, her voice musical. Her smile widened and there was the hint of pointed teeth at the corners of her mouth. And a hint of recognition. "Welcome to Tretower Castle."

"Tretower Castle?" Travaale said.

Ceara smiled. "We are but a moment out of time, my friend," she replied. "Soon you shall know all."

3

Travaale stood before a large ornately framed oval mirror mounted on a stone wall in a room. The room was spacious. And bare. A large ornate wooden table with two ornately carved high back chairs was the only furnishing. And two torches mounted in wall sconces. The flame of a nearby torch played across Travaale's features. He studied his face as his fingers lightly touched his long white hair. His short milky white beard had grown from unremembered days of wandering. His thoughts turned to the things Ceara had just spoken of, strange places and names he didn't recognize.

"I don't know these things of which you speak," Travaale said softly, watching himself in the mirror. He turned, his eyes coming to rest on Ceara. "Powys, Usk, Tretower, Radnor Forest...what does all this have to do with me?"

"You have come in answer to my summons," Ceara said.

"You bewitched me?"

Ceara smiled. "Bewitched," she muttered. Her eyes were staring and distant. Suddenly she turned her eyes to Travaale. Her smile widened. "I've been called many things – consort, concubine, wife, mother, devil's daughter, the wraith of Radnor Forest, the witch of

Tretower. But it was Batel Shamir that made me what I truly am now. A prisoner here."

"Explain."

Spite suddenly jumped out of the shadows, onto the table, and slowly waddled from one side of the table to the other and sat.

"This is where the roads of time cross," Ceara began. "The past, present, and future all come together. It's one of many such places."

While Travaale sat quietly at the table and listened, Ceara slowly paced about the room, telling her story. Batel Shamir was as old as time. He had risen in the desert wastes beyond an ancient city called Ur. An evil ancient curse, in his true form he was a bloated green worm. And death and pestilence traveled in his wake. It was said that his gaze would cut diamonds and shatter stone. It was true. Ceara had witnessed such. But in his human form, an avatar to walk amidst humanity, he was a thing of greed, envy, and wanton desire. He was compulsive and power mad, and his wanton desire had once been directed at Ceara.

She paused and chuckled. "His ultimate desire is to destroy Vergama," she said softly.

"Insanity," Travaale said. There was a pause; Ceara remained silent, and Travaale added, "You said he made you a prisoner here."

She nodded. "Yes," her voice soft as she continued her story. Shamir had called her to the castle ruins from a parallel time and then placed a ring of stones around the castle. They were a circle of slate gray stones as tall as a man that stood in a time where the castle didn't exist. Yet they were there, unseen by Ceara. They were magic stones whose power entrapped her. To pass beyond the ring of stones would destroy her. Their high pitched tone emitted across time and space warned Ceara of their presence. Only when the tone ceased would Ceara know their power had been negated and she was free.

"I hear no such tone," Travaale said.

"And you shant," Ceara replied. "Only I can hear it."

There was a soft squeal from Spite, and a snorted ring of soot.

"And Spite, of course," Ceara added.

"Again, what does this have to do with me?" Travaale said.

Ceara remained silent as she walked to the oval mirror and stared into it. There was no reflection. "I want you to destroy Shamir," she finally said, her back to Travaale. She paused then turned to Travaale. "The power of the stones lies with him. If he is destroyed, the stones lose their power and I'm set free."

"If he's as old as time as you say, and has powers to transcend time and space, how can he be destroyed?"

"Catch him unaware while he's in human form," Ceara replied. "He still retains his powers, but he also has all the frailties that humans possess. Strike him down before he can react."

Travaale slowly rose from the table and approached Ceara. A strange feeling came over him. He had been here at these ruins before, had already spoken with Ceara, had already confronted Batel Shamir. All these things, all these events had happened before. And Travaale now knew they would happen again. Ceara's request couldn't be refused. Travaale had already accepted, long before, and would again. Many times. He was cursed. It would be a cycle he would repeat.

"Alright," he said softly, without question.

"There's no time to lose," Ceara replied, her voice soft and alluring. "You must return to your own time and place."

4

"You'll know him by his snake eyes," Ceara was saying as she, Travaale, and the little soot snorting beast made their way down the shadow darkened black stone corridor. "Remember to beware his gaze; he can shatter stone and cause walls to crumble."

The little soot snorting beast was leading the way. Here there was no firelight, no wall sconces, no torches. Only an occasion slit in the wall in the shape of a cross. *Defenses,* Ceara had explained. Travaale had felt her eyes on him, cold and powerful. Yet soft when she wished to be. He glanced at her, saw her eyes sparkle as they passed a shaft of light cutting in the defense opening. A ghost-like wraith in the soft temporary light, she grinned and continued –

"He travels from town to town, city to city, taking what he needs to sustain himself," Ceara explained. "There are few left in your world, and fewer still in Oroth. That's where you'll find him - at the Zharanet Estate."

"How do you know these things?" Travaale questioned.

She smiled. "I see them."

Of that Travaale had no doubt. Ceara could see far beyond the mere shadows of the corridor they walked. Just what else could she see? And do? She claimed that Shamir possessed strange and evil powers. Travaale was convinced that Ceara was not free of such powers herself.

"Shamir has a servant as protector; his name is Lek Duulan." Ceara added. "Watch for him; he's human, but still dangerous."

She stopped before a great oaken door and passed a hand over a rusted padlock. The lock fell open. The door slowly creaked open on its own, on a dream world that Travaale hardly knew. He paused and stared, hesitant, somewhat fearful. Blue sky, tiny yellow sun, green vegetation. It was a sight to behold. Certainly nothing like his home, the desolate and dusty Zothique. This world of blue, yellow, and green was ancestral to Travaale's world, but a time far removed, a time that would never come again. And soon desolate Zothique would be gone just as the blue, yellow and green world had gone.

Travaale stepped through the door and turned to face Ceara. She had been smiling, and the smile had suddenly turned to a frown. There was a darkness to come that even she couldn't escape. She saw a future that Travale couldn't see, a darkness at the end of days. And she would be there.

"Your thoughts are troubled," Travaale said simply.

"The end of all things is near," Ceara replied.

"The end isn't long in coming to my world," Travaale said.

"In your world the end has already begun. It's written in the *Book of Destiny*." Ceara paused, glanced at the sunshine streaming through the trees then turned her eyes to the wanderer from Izdrel. "Farewell, Zan Travaale."

"Farewell," Travaale said. "And farewell my little soot snorting friend." He turned and started to walk away.

"Travaale!" Ceara called out.

He stopped and turned.

"Just before Shamir dies, give him my regards," she said softly. Her eyes were cold and staring.

Travaale nodded and turned away, his thoughts on his recent experience. This new wondrous land, the little soot snorting beast, the standing stones around the ruins in another time, Batel Shamir – all this and more he accepted. He deemed it sorcerous. It'd been sorcery that had brought him to this place. And this woman. All she had said, he had listened, and had accepted her honesty. But what *of* this woman so mysterious? What was the truth about her?

Part way across the courtyard of the ruined tower Travaale paused. He turned and stared silently back at the woman in the doorway, the little soot snorting beast prancing about her feet. "Tell me, Ceara," he finally said, "who are you?"

She waited, perhaps a moment, perhaps less then smiled with a tilt of her head. "I'm the first woman," she said simply, and cryptically she added, "and I shall be the last."

It wasn't an answer that Travaale understood. First woman and last. Ever the mystery. Without expression, without a word, Travaale stared a moment longer then turned and continued on his way.

Ceara watched as he left the courtyard, rounded a corner, and was gone. "May Mordiggian look after you, Travaale," she said softly. Though a light shown in her eyes, there was something dark there, dark in her thoughts. And malevolent. She chuckled softly as she turned and disappeared into the round tower ruins.

*   *   *

It had been a nightmare. The demon worm Shamir had killed Ceara. The worm was a bloated green thing, as long as a man is tall. It moved on hundreds of tiny cilia-like legs. Six long snake-like tentacles writhed in the air, three to each side. Jagged sharp teeth lined a round maw just below two bulbous eyes.

Ceara had stood motionless on the path, oblivious to the creature. She'd done nothing to save herself. The thing had reared up behind her, wrapped its tentacles about her then sank its teeth into the back of her skull.

Tissue shredded, bones cracked, blood poured down her back. Her eyelids fluttered. Only for a moment. And then her eyes were sucked out of the gaping hole in the back of her skull along with her brain and the upper half of her spinal chord. The demon worm had released her; she had fallen face first onto the path. The worm was gone, disappeared into the dense underbrush.

Travaale awakened from the nightmare, reached for his saber, and sat up. His eyes were wide, his heart raced, and he sucked in air. More for the nightmare than the thin atmosphere of his desolate home. The night was gone and the day had come. The bloated red sun was rising in the orange sky. All about was the barren blasted landscape of Celotia. A slight wind whistled down a nearby canyon cleft. Dust devils swirled across the rock and desert pavement. There was no blue sky, no green foliage, no tiny yellow sun. *A dream?* Travaale thought. He shook his head. *No, not a dream.* Travaale was home. He jumped to his feet, gathered his meager belongings, and hurried off toward Oroth.

5

As Travaale approached the south gate of the Zharanet Estate, he grinned, an inner light smoldering deep in his eyes, an inner darkness welling up within him. This would be a moment of action – as quick as possible, deliberate, and…deadly. The demon worm would be destroyed. A dark brooding took over his smile. He let out a short curt laugh. Holding his saber pointed at the ground, Travaale crossed the grounds to the estate's garden entrance.

"You can't go in there." It was a guard in a corridor outside the banquet hall.

"You just watch," came Travaale's reply as he pushed the guard aside and kept walking.

It was a gathering of the high-officials of Oroth come to decide a course to save the dying city. A murmur of discussion reverberated about the dim banquet hall. There was a sudden hush as the voice of the guard echoed in the adjacent corridor. All eyes focused on the man who burst into the room, his saber drawn. His eyes were dark and brooding, hinting at an inner darkness that sent chills through several of those gathered.

Corod Valdhari stood nearby, a hand resting on the pummel of his sword. "What is the meaning of this? Who are you that…"

"Who let this vagabond barbarian in?" a man said sternly, cutting off Valdhari. The man took a step toward Travaale.

Travaale turned and raised his saber to the stranger.

The man, eyes wide with uncertainty, stepped back a step.

After a cursory glance about the room, Travaale turned his eyes back to the stranger. "Sir, I don't believe I know you." His words short, threatening.

"Lek Duulan," the stranger replied. "What gives you the right to barge in here?"

"Do you now speak for the House of Zharanet?" Travaale said coldly, raising the saber higher.

"I speak for the House of Zharanet," came a woman's voice. Eyes turned. Shenja Zharanet's tone belayed all uncertainty as to who was in charge. Her countenance was strong, eyes piercing; she glared at Travaale as she approached. "Who are you? What is your business here? And lower that saber!"

Travaale smiled and nodded. "As you wish," he replied. He lowered the sword, but kept it drawn, pointed to the floor. "I'm Zan Travaale of Izdrel."

"Travaale?" Valdhari questioned as he stepped from the shadows.

Travaale turned to his old friend and smiled.

"I thought I recognized that voice of yours," Valdhari continued, clapping the wanderer from Izdrel on the shoulder. "It's been years. What brings you to Oroth?"

"There's demon among you," Travaale replied, loud enough for all to hear.

"How would you know this?" Shenja said as she joined Travaale and Valdhari.

"I came here at the bidding of a lady from another...land," Travaale said softly.

A murmur suddenly erupted around the room.

"And who is this lady that you speak of?" said a small snake-eyed man that had suddenly appeared out of the shadows.

Travaale turned and stared. There was no doubt. It was in the man's eyes. This was he. Batel Shamir. The curse of the worm. This was the man who'd trapped Ceara in the ruins of Castle Tretower. "I'm sure you know, Batel Shamir," Travaale replied.

"Ridiculous!" Duulan erupted, turning to Shenja. "This barbarian comes here with tales of demons…"

Zharanet raised a hand and Duulan fell silent. "Do you have any proof of your claims?" she questioned Travaale.

Travaale ignored Zharanet. He tightened his grip on the hilt of his saber. There was darkness in him, rising and spreading. He cackled as he eyed Shamir, and a cold and dark grin crawled across his face. "I shall show you your proof," Travaale finally said, his eyes locked on Shamir.

Shamir knew the confrontation was unavoidable. The iris' of his snake eyes narrowed as he sneered at the wanderer from Izdrel and began his transformation. The transformation was rapid. It took everyone by surprise. The snake-eyed man became the demon worm. The thing hissed as it reared up and lunged forward to feed, clasping the nearest victim which happened to be Lek Duulan. Writhing tentacles wrapped around the protector of the worm. With a gurgling hiss the thing sank its circle of jagged teeth into the back of Duulan's skull. The skull cracked; a tearing of flesh; Duulan screamed. The demon worm sucked Duulan's blood, spinal fluid, brain, spinal column, and eyes through the hole in the back of his head.

Mass confusion of those gathered sent people scurrying about the large room. It was enough, along with its feeding on Duulan, to blind Shamir from Travaale's slow and cautious approached. Travaale gripped his saber, ready to swing and cut down the demon worm. Then the worm saw, and swung its head. Its eyes flashed and a corner of the ceiling exploded in crumbling stone. Ceara had been right. Its eyes could cut through stone.

The demon worm's tentacles threw the now lifeless body of Duulan against a wall. Its head swung around again, eyes searching for Travaale, eyes tearing a long jagged gash through another wall as the terrified townspeople dove for cover. Travaale had gained the advantage, had slipped behind the demon worm. The wanderer from Izdrel lunged at Shamir and clung to its bulbous mass with one arm as the worm bucked to dislodge him. And with saber in free hand, Travaale reached around and shoved the point of his saber through the demon worm's right eye and into its brain.

"Ceara sends her regards," Travaale grunted as he ground the blade of his saber into Shamir's brain.

The demon worm howled. It reared back, its remaining good eye tearing at the ceiling, sending fragmented stone raining down on those gathered. Travaale was thrown clear. He caught himself, rolled to his feet, and crouched with saber ready. There was no need for defense. The demon worm's one good eye dimmed. No longer did it cut through stone. With a hissing gasp and flailing of its tentacles, the demon worm crashed to the floor, green ichor oozing from the eye wound. It breathed a raspy breath then fell silent.

Travaale sighed as he stared at Shamir. His thoughts reflected to another time and place. "You're free now," he muttered under his breath then turned and left the ruined banquet hall as those gathered slowly wandered about, wide-eyed, staring at the dead thing on the floor. Only the clicking of Travaale's heels interrupted the silence.

The silence remained after the wanderer from Izdrel was gone. "Somebody please remove...this...thing," Shenja Zharanet finally said, breaking the silence, gesturing with a wave of her hand.

* * *

The high pitched siren-like tone slowly faded and was gone. The demon worm was dead. The wanderer from Izdrel had succeeded. Ceara was free to roam the earth again as she had for untold ages before being imprisoned by Batel Shamir. Shamir had feared death, and had vowed to live until the end, feeding off the life, flesh, and blood of others. And the demon worm had feared the power of death that was manifest in Ceara. It knew there were others like her, but only Ceara had lived so long and had been the first woman. The demon worm couldn't take chances. But in the end, Ceara, the first woman, had won.

With a cackling laugh of triumph, a gleam in her eyes, and darkness in her soul, Ceara left the ruins of Castle Tretower forever. The little soot snorting beast had followed her, and together they traveled through time and space, Ceara feeding off others to sustain herself in much the same manner that Shamir had. Somewhere in time the little soot snorting beast died, something Ceara could not do. She continued on through time, nation to nation, land to land – feeding, killing, sustaining her existence, vowing to be the last.

One day a small boat left a southerly island. The boat brought Ceara to a new land. This new land was the last continent. It was called Zothique. She smiled as she stepped ashore. The world, at long last, was entering its twilight.

* * *

Travaale left the house by the same way he'd entered. In the ruined garden he paused and rested his back against a stone wall. Killing Shamir was easier than he'd thought it would be. *Or maybe I was just lucky,* he thought, breathing a sigh of relief. A shadow suddenly fluttered past his head. He turned and looked, but whatever it had been, it was gone. *Ceara. Passing from captivity.* It was an odd thought, but it was the first that had come to mind.

"Travaale!" The voice came from behind, a quick shout.

The voice belonged to Valdhari. Travaale turned and saw his old friend standing at the garden entrance. Valdhari stared. He was puzzled. Travaale looked back at him, expressionless.

Then Valdhari grinned. "You're leaving us so soon," Valdhari said as he approached his old friend. "I can see it in your eyes."

"You know me well," Travaale chuckled. "I can't stay in any one place too long."

Valdhari's expression changed. He was contemplative, hesitant. He glanced at the ground at his feet then at his old friend. "Who's this woman that sent you here?" he questioned softly.

"She's an old friend, Corod." Zan Travaale smiled. "A very old friend."

The Dying Shall Die

1

Senedgian's eyes flared as he jumped up from his makeshift throne made of an amalgamation of human bones. "You sure? Absolutely?"

Nailok nodded. "It was him," he replied softly, stepping back, uneasy at Senedgian's thunderous outburst. His eyes widened.

Senedgian stepped down from his throne. Self-proclaimed King of Darcor, he glared deep into Nailok's eyes. Nailok caught his breath. Senedgian was imposing. He stood nearly seven feet tall, wore a leather vest, and leather belts crisscrossed his chest. The pearl handle of a dagger, sheathed on the side of his right boot, glistened in the dull light of the smoky crumbling tavern that Senedgian had appropriated for his palace. The knee high leather boots clicked on the stone floor as Senedgian moved his great bulk.

A scar crossed Senedgian's right cheek; an eye patch covered his right eye; long matted hair was laced with gray and thinning at the top of his head. Senedgian had a reputation. He wasn't to be crossed. And those that did generally wound up dead. When not a swift, spur of the moment, fit of rage dead, it would be a slow agonizing painful death deviously devised by Senedgian. And it hadn't taken long for him to kill off most of Darcor's population. Of course, there hadn't been many left. Now only the chief magistrate and his wife were still alive. They might just as well have been dead.

No one knew where Senedgian came from. There were a myriad of rumors, but they all traced back to a common thread – his mother a Zul-Bha-Sair harlot and his father none other than Mordiggian. *A demigod,* people would whisper. And Senedgian would only smile, keeping his secret.

"No one double cross Senedgian," the King of Darcor growled then shouted, his rage icy and lethal – "No One!" He paused, stared with a fire in his eyes then added, his voice a soft growl, "And that include Dal Seerco." He spun on his heels, his eyes glaring, cutting through the shadowed tavern before falling upon Nailok. "Where Gallen and Kaasher?"

"Fo...following Seerco," Nailok stammered. "In eastern Celotia. He moves east toward..."

"Chaon Gacca," Senedgian interrupted. "A good place for him to die." He chuckled, his eyes staring and distant then turned to Nailok once again. "Ready my mount while I kill magistrate and his wife." The self-proclaimed King of Darcor hurried from the tavern by way of a back door.

* * *

The magistrate of Darcor and his wife hung naked from the ceiling of the government building's conference room, their bodies partially flayed, blood pooling on the dusty floor. Delirious, barely conscious, barely alive, yet they moaned moreso from the weight placed on their bound and blackened wrists.

Senedgian crossed the debris strewn floor to the conference table that had been pushed aside. There was a wooden box on the table that contained six firebugs. Senedgian had placed them there the night before, knowing that there would soon be occasion to use them. The firebugs were as long as a man's hand, had sharp three-pronged pinchers, and secreted an acidic enzyme that reduced flesh to an oozing mass of slime fit for the firebugs to pluck with the pinchers and ingest. It was an exceedingly slow and painful process as attested by the howling screams of those who had the misfortune to being consumed by firebugs.

"Six firebugs," Senedgian chuckled as he picked up the box and tongs lying on the table next to the box. One never picked up a firebug with your fingers. "That three for you and three for you," hc said, nodding to each in turn.

Howling with delighted amusement, Senedgian lifted the box lid, plucked out a firebug with the tongs, and placed it against the partially flayed leg of the magistrate. The firebug went to work, and the magistrate began to howl. Senedgian howled louder, delighted at the magistrate's pain. It wouldn't be long before the firebugs would kill them both.

* * *

The agonized howling of the magistrate and his wife echoed down the deserted rubble strewn street. Nailok flinched at the sound. His thoughts drifted to the night he'd spent with the magistrate's wife. Senedgian had thought it profitable to rent her out to interested customers at a price of 8 *curats*. To his close friends and associates, the cost had only been 4 *curats*. As more and more of the townsfolk were horribly slaughtered, it became less profitable, and the magistrate's wife ended up hanging from the ceiling next to her already tortured husband.

The sound of howling pain made the two dromedaries uneasy. They shifted on their feet, prancing, snorting. Nailok held fast to the reins, trying to steady them as he awaited Senedgian. Finally, the self-proclaimed King of Darcor appeared. The magistrate and his wife would soon be dead. Senedgian and Nailok were leaving town. In a matter of a few short hours, Darcor would be abandoned and left to the harsh elements. A dead town in a dying world.

Senedgian walked with a scowl on his face, a glare in his one good eye, kicking debris out of his path. From his waist belt hung the scabbard of his great broadsword, a sword no normal man could wield. His hand rested lightly on the pearled hilt of the great sword, a hilt matching the pearled handle of the dagger he sported in his boot. He tore the reins of his beast from Nailok's hand, and the two men mounted their dromedaries.

"I look forward to see Seerco again," Senedgian growled, his voice cold and dark. "But Seerco not like to see me!" He roared with laughter as he and Nailok turned in the alley and rode away.

No more needed to be said, for the moment.

* * *

The sun had just set. It was blood red on the horizon. The desolate plateau was windswept and dust devils swirled across the bleak landscape. A troubled Dal Seerco stood silent upon the plateau near its edge, unmoving, his thoughts far away to the southwest and the dying lawless town of Darcor. It'd been years since he'd fled Darcor, but the town still haunted him. He knew instinctively that Darcor had at last died. The last of its inhabitants, Senedgian and Nailok had left. And they were coming for him.

Out of the shadows of jagged boulders stepped Nalia, a tall pale woman of regal bearing. Lightly stepping, she quietly joined Seerco upon the plateau. The evening air was cooling, and Nalia pulled tighter the cloak she wore about her shoulders.

"I sense something bothers you," she said, a light in her eyes.

"They're coming," he replied, his eyes scanning the desolate landscape.

"Who?"

"I don't know."

But he knew.

* * *

A small cluster of ruined thatched huts were huddled haphazardly on a narrow river bench, nestled in a canyon and cut off from the howling winds and blinding sand of desolate Celotia. The huts had been hastily thrown together as a place to stay until the end of the world. They knew it was coming, the five men and four women who had founded their little village in order to serve their god and await the end of the world.

They were all that was left of a group of religious zealots called Eshuneans in honor of their ancient god whom they called Eshu. They were chaste, renouncing the flesh, giving absolute devotion in mind, body, and spirit to their god. Then Kaasher and Gallen had come amidst them. Three of the four women were no longer chaste.

Only the elderly woman who sat rocking in a chair in a darkened corner of one of the huts remained chaste.

It's a test of our faith! one of the Eshu devotees had cried.

Eshu has sent us to guide you! Kaasher had decreed with a salacious eye turned upon one of the four women. *Our words are the words and will of Eshu!* And the smile on the face of this Holy Messenger of Eshu widened expectantly.

The believers couldn't refuse the will and testament of their god. It was Eshu's will that the Eshunean men turn over their women to these two newcomers, these Holy Messengers. Except, of course, for the elderly woman in the corner. Eshu preferred that she remain comfortable, in her chair, in the corner. Left alone. So said the Holy Messenger who called himself Kaasher.

So it had been for two weeks while the Holy Messengers had stayed amongst the followers of Eshu. They had come, said the Holy Messenger who called himself Kaasher, in search of an agent of evil, a demon of the evil god Mordiggian.

Mordiggian is a false god! the faithful had cried.

When we bring the demon Seerco before Eshu, the truth shall be known and the demon destroyed! proclaimed the Holy Messenger who called himself Gallen. *For now, we watch his movements.*

The Eshunean faithful shuddered at the mention of the evil demon Seerco. Surely he must be powerful. They waited. Again it was time to see to the demon. This time the Holy Messenger Gallen would go forth on foot.

The shadows had long crawled over the edge of the canyon. Above, the sky was a deep red, tending to blood red. Night was coming. The two Holy Messengers stood outside a hut that was barely standing. One stiff wind howling through the canyon and it would fall. It was the House of Eshu, the place where the Eshuneans worshipped their god.

"I'm going up the ravine, make sure Seerco hasn't slipped away on us," Gallen said, slinging a pack over his shoulder. "The night'll give me cover."

"Won't be long 'fore Nailok gets back with Senedgian," Kaasher replied. "A couple days maybe. We'll catch up."

Gallen slapped Kaasher on the shoulder and smiled. "You keep those wenches warm."

"I'm about to warm one up right now," Kaasher laughed. "It's the will of Eshu, you know."

They roared with laughter as Gallen turned away and disappeared down the ravine. Kaasher watched until Gallen was gone from sight then turned and swung open the door of the House of Eshu. Inside all eyes turned to the Holy Messenger as he stuck his head in the door. He ignored the men and the old woman. His eyes scanned the three remaining women. The choice was made. He grinned.

"You," Kaasher said, pointing to a young woman standing in the shadows. "It's your turn. Come."

Dutifully, obeying the will of Eshu, she left the hut with the Holy Messenger Kaasher.

* * *

Dim stars lit the night sky over Zothique. They were old stars in an old sky draped over an old world that was dying. Still, the game of life was to be played out in its lust, desire, and wanton destruction.

Nalia sat cross-legged before a natural circular depression in the stone of a rock outcropping amidst jagged boulders thrusting at the night. A thin layer of dust covered the depression, blown in by the night wind between the jagged boulders. Nalia stared into the depression while her mind's eye stared into space, back to the small wooden thatched roof hut she and Seerco shared. Seerco remained asleep while Nalia's projection sat nearby in case he should awaken unexpectedly.

Satisfied, she passed a hand over the depression. It rippled like water, smoked over then cleared. An image had formed. Two men seated at a campfire. One demure and snake-like, the other hulking and brutish. Again she passed a hand over the depression, and again it smoked then cleared on a new image. It was another man – sharing a bed with a young woman.

"An Eshunean woman," Nalia whispered to herself.

She grinned, laughed, and passed a hand over the depression once again. The image smoked and cleared. A new image was formed.

This time a man camped on the edge of a ravine. No campfire to betray him. *Must be close,* Nalia thought. *Perhaps too close.*

Passing a hand over the depression again, no new image formed. Only the dust lined rock depression remained. Nalia sat back and sighed. "Four," she said softly, smiling as she stared into the night.

* * *

Nestled between boulders, Gallen was waiting for the sun to rise. Across the ravine was a small hut. Seerco and the woman who traveled with him were staying there. Gallen grinned in the dark, eyes scanning the outline of the hut. It was dark there. No firelight. *Maybe they gone,* he thought then brushed it off. His thoughts turned to the woman that traveled with Seerco. He and Kaasher had spotted them together a few days before, standing atop a bluff. She was tall with long cascading hair that rode on the wind like an old time galley sail. Seerco is to die, Gallen knew. But the woman…

Gallen caught his breath as he ducked. There was a torch in the night, weaving between the boulders. The torchlight skirted the other side of the ravine then was gone. Quickly. *Seerco?* Gallen wondered. He didn't know. But the thought of being alone in the dark with Seerco unnerved him. He crouched, still, silent, hoping that whoever it was, they'd pass by and Gallen would remain undetected. Slowly he turned and crouched on his knees, peering from behind a boulder across the ravine. Still the torchlight was gone. There was silence and stillness in the night. And Gallen breathed a sigh of relief as he turned and sat back against the boulder.

The movement of shadow caught Gallen's eye. Something was there, coming nearer. his eyes went wide with momentary fear then softened with recognition. A sly smile suddenly crawled across his face as he began to rise to his feet.

2

They were all gathered in the House of Eshu. The nine Eshuneans along with Kaasher, Nailok, and Senedgian. All eyes watched the big man as he paced the floor, his one good eye scanning the eyes of the

Eshuneans, his boot heels clicking in the otherwise silent morning. The big man eyed the Eshuneanas maliciously, but they showed no fear. Eshu would protect them. It had indeed been a test of their faith, they knew. The men called Kaasher and Gallen had not been Holy Messengers of Eshu. They were evil, in league with Mordiggian like the demon man called Seerco they claimed to be pursuing. And should this big man do them harm, then it was the will of Eshu, and they would bask in the glorious eternal light of their god.

For a brief moment Senedgian entertained the idea of nine new subjects to persecute, torture, and murder. But the black cloud called Seerco passed through his thoughts. Senedgian would forego the persecution and torture. Murder would be the order of the day. Seerco's death just couldn't wait. The double-crossing traitor was far too important for Senedgian to be wasting time with these nine weak minded religious zealots.

In a fit of rage, Seerco taunting his thoughts, Senedgian grabbed the nearest Eshunean, a young man, and raked the blade of his dagger across the neck of the young follower of the ancient god. Blood spurted from his neck. Eyes wide, he gurgled and gasped as Senedgian released him. The young man dropped to his knees then collapsed to the floor. Senedgian glared at the dead man while Nailok and Kaasher chuckled from the shadows of the hut.

"Sir, I must protes....," an elderly Eshunean man began as he stepped forward.

Senedgian lunged at the man, cutting him off, pushing him back and laying him flat out on a table. Two quick thrusts of the knife took out the man's eyes then a slashing of his throat took out his life. Two lives given for Eshu.

The remaining seven Eshuneans followed the fate of the first two. Slaughtered, their throats slashed, decorative designs carved into a few according Senedgian's whim. With the blood and bodies of the last of the Eshuneans adorning the interior of the House of Eshu, Senedgian and his henchmen set fire to the house of worship and the remaining squalid huts. Black smoke rolled into the pink sky of early morning. It could be seen for miles across Celotia.

"Now I kill Seerco," Senedgian growled as the three of them sat atop their dromedaries. "Come." He nudged his dromedary and started down the ravine in the same direction that Gallen had gone on foot the night before. Kaasher and Nailok followed, Kaasher leading Gallen's dromedary along with them.

* * *

Black smoke billowed into the morning sky. It was southwest, along the ravine, less than a day's ride. But Seerco and Nalia were on foot. *They* would be riding. Still, it was of no concern to Seerco. He and Nalia would have time. They were headed toward Chaon Gacca. If there was any kind of perverse justice, Seerco knew that Senedgian would try to intercept him there. A fitting place for a showdown.

"The Eshuneans?" Nalia questioned as she and Seerco stood in front of their squalid shack and watched the black cloud billow into the morning sky.

"Yes," Seerco voiced softly and nodded.

"Those that you spoke of last night?"

"Yes," Seerco repeated, again nodding. He turned to Nalia and added, "They'll stop at nothing...kill anyone who gets in their way."

"These people are coming after you," Nalia said.

"Yes, they are," Seerco replied.

"What did you do..." Nalia began.

Seerco cut her off as he turned toward their shack. "No time to explain now. Let's gather what we can carry and leave."

Nalia stared as he disappeared into the shack then followed.

They gathered together what they could carry in two leather shoulder packs; anything else would have to be left behind. Seerco torched the shack. *To let them know we know they're coming,* he had said when Nalia wondered if it was wise to give away their location. With the bloated morning red sun hanging low in the eastern sky, Seerco and Nalia slipped away, skirting boulders and rocks, keeping to cover, they made their way northeast toward the ruined ghost town and former capital of Tasuun, Chaon Gacca.

* * *

Is he dead?

It had been a stupid question. Kaasher had asked it, his voice soft and shaken. Of course Gallen was dead. Naked and hanging by his feet from a rope draped around the top of a tall boulder, he was gutted and his throat had been ripped out. Gallen was certainly dead. Senedgian had dismounted, stood half way between his dromedary and the dead body. He grumbled angrily under his breath as his eyes narrowed and focused on the near future that saw him gutting Seerco as Seerco had gutted Gallen.

"Kaasher," Senedgian growled angrily as his eyes turned to the column of smoke that rose from the consumed ruins of the shack across the ravine. "Ride. Find Seerco; soften him up. But don't kill. I kill Seerco myself."

"Seerco...di...did this..."

"Go now or I kill you!" Senedgian shouted at the fearful Kaasher.

Kaasher hurriedly pulled the reins of his dromedary, turning it away from the others. He was off down the ravine, skirting boulders, rocks, and crevices, the hoofs of the dromedary kicking up dust. With each trot his nerve began to return. Seerco, he couldn't be all that bad. He had fled Darcor, fled Senedgian. He was afraid and was now on the run. Kaasher chuckled with his growing confidence.

* * *

This place wasn't Chaon Gacca. It was an outlier, a satellite shanty town of ramshackle wooden structures – ruined, diseased, a hovel where the disease had killed everything. Much smaller than Chaon Gacca, the shanty town, its name long forgotten, was little more than a cluster of crumbling huts along a dirt and dusty main street with few side alleys. And it was the only town along this desolate stretch that led to Tasuun's former capital.

Long dead and decayed bodies were strewn about as though some disease had taken them and they died where they'd fallen. Some appeared to have met a violent end, bodies hanging from poles, nailed spread eagle to walls, skeletons showing violent damage. Death was everywhere, but strangely there was no sense of death, no feeling. Just one of extreme age to a crumbling shanty town that was on the verge of being reclaimed by nature.

At the end of the dusty narrow main street, Seerco stopped and slowly began to turn. The dead were all about, but it was the living Seerco had suddenly felt. Nalia glanced at him then turned her eyes as well. Around a bend at the opposite end of the town a rider appeared. He slowed his dromedary then stopped.

"Seerco!" the man shouted, his eyes darting between Seerco and Nalia. The stranger dismounted and drew his sword. The sword sang of ringing metal. His manner of dress was of a Darcorian thief.

"I'm Dal Seerco," Seerco's voice was soft. "Do I know you, sir?"

"Kaasher," the man replied, a little hesitant. But a grin crawled across his face as he added, "In service to Senedgian of Darcor." Kaasher's eyes darted from Seerco's waist belt to Nalia then back to Seerco. "I see you're unarmed."

"I haven't had the need to arm myself," Seerco replied. A coldness from a former life suddenly flared in his eyes.

"Until now," Kaasher said.

"You come to kill me?" Seerco's said. "I, an unarmed man?"

"Alive or dead," Kaasher said. "It makes no difference to me."

"I know Senedgian well," Seerco called out with a grin. "He would prefer me alive."

With sword poised to strike, Kaasher started down the street toward Seerco and Nalia.

In the face of confrontation, Seerco's thoughts gave way to his blackened past. Cold indifference entered his heart and shown in his eyes. It was a moment of survival. Instinct for self-preservation took over. *Kill or be killed,* he thought. He knew he could never escape his past. Seerco grinned. If Kaasher persisted, he was walking to his impending death.

Kaasher suddenly noted something in Seerco's expression – the sneering grin, the piercing eyes. It was enough to unnerve him, and the Darcor thief stopped in the middle of the street. A darkness crept over Kaasher and a feeling of impending doom.

"What are you?" Kaasher cried, taking a step backward as the darkness spread.

"I give you your life," Seerco called out in a rare moment of mercy. "Take it and go!"

Kaasher remained silent, staring, and slowly lowered his sword. The darkness that shrouded his thoughts taunted him. There was death in that shroud of black, and it was Kaasher's own.

"Come, let's leave, quickly," Seerco said, taking Nalia by the hand. His eyes never wavered from Kaasher. It puzzled Seerco why Kaasher had suddenly stopped in the middle of the street. It was evident that something had frightened Kaasher. Seerco saw it in his eyes. But what? Seerco shrugged as he and Nalia turned and hurried out of town, leaving Kaasher surrounded by the darkness that was closing in around him.

"Why are they trying to kill you?" Nalia questioned as they fled the crumbling shanty town.

"I have a reputation that likes to follow me," Seerco replied. "I had thought to be rid of it."

"What kind of reputation?"

"Not a good one."

Nalia let it go, and turned her thoughts instead to the dusty shanty town main street they'd just left.

* * *

The black cloud swirled in Kaasher's thoughts. Strange cries of pain, anguish, and terror echoed through his mind. Suddenly the cloud and cries were gone. A soft breeze whistled. Little eddies of dust danced in the street. Nearby something creaked, wind against wood. There was a shadow of movement that stopped. Kaasher slowly turned in the street. And grinned.

"Now what do we have here?" he said expectantly.

* * *

Nailok sat atop his dromedary in the middle of the dusty street. His heart was racing, his eyes wide and darting to every creaking board buffeted by the wind. Senedgian had dismounted. He stared at the severed head in the middle of the street then slowly approached. It was Kaasher's head, sitting upright, staring through dead eyes. His body was no where to be seen.

"Seerco did it," Nailok whined fearfully.

Senedgian ignored him. In a fit of rage, he kicked Kaasher's head. It bounced off the front of a clapboard building that teetered on the brink of disaster, rolled across a rotting wooden sidewalk and back into the street. Hands clenched in fists, Senedgian howled in rage at the top of his lungs. Without a word, he remounted his dromedary. The two men left the crumbling shanty town.

3

The campfire crackled. A dromedary snorted. Senedgian snorted. His eye glistened in the firelight as he stared into the dancing flames. But in his mind's eye, he saw not the flames but the dead and mutilated body of Dal Seerco. And the mind sight caused a slow grin to spread across his face.

A sudden snap and shower of embers caused Nailok to jump. He was on edge, nervous and frightened. His eyes darted to the dark of night that surrounded them, a veil of darkness that was closing in tighter as the fire dwindled. And there wasn't anymore scrap wood within a mile to replenish it.

A catch of breath, and Nailok turned his eyes to the surrounding dark. Strange cries echoed out of the night. Horrible beasts? Dying people? Or Seerco taunting them? Nailok shivered and turned his gaze to Senedgian to find the last King of Darcor grinning at him, a strange eerie light in his one good eye. Nailok didn't like the look on Senedgian's face.

"Oh no...n...," Nailok was stammering as he began to push away. He knew what the self-proclaimed King of Darcor had in mind.

Senedgian grabbed Nailok by the arm and dragged him close, nearly rolling him through the campfire. "You find Seerco," Senedgian growled. "Then I come and kill him."

"But...but," Nailok was begging, "you sent Gallen and Kaasher, and he killed them!"

Senedgian laughed. "They afraid Seerco," he said. "You not afraid Seerco, right?"

Nailok tried to shake his head, but finally nodded. "He'll kill me just like he..."

Enraged, Senedgian back handed Nailok across the campfire. "You find Seerco! Or I kill you myself! Go!"

Nailok scrambled to his feet and hurried to his tethered dromedary. His eyes darted between the dark of night and the eerie campfire glow on Senedgian's face as he freed the reins and mounted. Without a word, Nailok reined his dromedary around and disappeared into the night while Senedgian turned his empty gaze back to the campfire.

* * *

Seerco stared into the campfire and focused on events of the past. They were events that had led to this day, this moment. There had been an alley in Darcor, a gathering of people. They had come to listen to a man who had spoken out against Senedgian. This man had been a rival of the self-proclaimed King of Darcor. And this man had been Seerco's first victim. His death had been ordered by Senedgian. It had been many years ago. The image was faint.

There had been others, so many others. Seerco focused on few, what he could remember in his clouded thoughts. The images were in no particular order, just images of death that Seerco had lauded in at one time. But no longer. More recent his profession had been forced upon him. He had tired of the killing. And now he wanted it finished. But as long as Senedgian and the others remained alive...

"They're going to have to die," Seerco muttered softly.

His thoughts turned darker, his heart to ice, his eyes black and cold. He flashed back, saw a boy running down a side alley in Darcor. The boy had lived off the streets, a street thief and vagabond drifting borough to borough, living and sleeping where he could. And he had become quite proficient at his trade. Senedgian had been impressed. He had taken the youth under his wing, a protégé. And the youth had grown up to become Seerco the assassin, and in time, the greatest assassin in all Darcor.

Murder, rape, thievery, coercion, slavery, a place where fires had raged constantly, and dark clouds of smoke had hung heavy over the city, never ending. This had been Darcor. The law had been the law of the jungle. Senedgian's law. Until he'd broken Senedgian's law. Until *that* night four years gone with Tarbo and Glys...

A snap of fire wood sent a shower of glowing embers into the night air, clouding Seerco's memories. He glanced at Nalia. She sat rigid, staring, her eyes distant. Seerco knew that her thoughts were elsewhere.

*   *   *

Night sounds echoed all around. Nailok's pace was slow and fearful. Cries in the dark broke down his defenses. A sudden cry and then cackling laughter caused him to draw up on the reins. The dromedary stopped. In the distance came another cry. It was a cry of pain and anguish like those of Darcor's unfortunate, like those in Darcor that Nailok and his compatriots had caused. Then, he had laughed; now, he shuddered.

Now there was silence. Nailok stared into the dark and held his breath, held his eyes wide. There was no sound, no movement. The dromedary suddenly snorted. It was restless and wanted to move on. A shadow suddenly passed. Nailok turned and saw.

There it was. A tall beast with female features. A she-bat. It stood two heads taller than Nailok, sported long fingers with claws, long black hair, softly glowing eyes that pierced the night, leathery wings now folded behind, and a mouth full of long jagged teeth. It slowly raised its clawed hands as it approached, and Nailok could have sworn that it winked at him.

A sudden howling hiss from the creature sent the dromedary to bucking. Nailok was thrown to the ground and the dromedary disappeared into the night. And as Nailok rolled over, the she-bat was upon him. The howling scream quickly became no more than a choking gurgle as the she-bat tore Nailok's throat out with its long jagged teeth and began to suck blood from the gaping wound.

The she-bat was quickly sated on the blood of Nailok's death. It dropped the body and peered into the dark, its eyes like gleaming beacons, renewed on blood, rejuvenated. A hissing howl erupted and echoed across the desolate landscape. Night creatures heard and shrunk back into the shadows and remained there – silent and still.

They stayed that way as the she-bat made its way through the night, hissing expectantly, a big man sitting at a campfire in its mind's eye.

It passed through the night in the near absolute darkness, the stars above dim in the sky, a combination of an aging universe and clouds of dust riding the night wind obscuring their light. Occasionally the she-bat's wings would flutter, lifting it over large boulders or across crevices and ravines. It didn't have far to go, and didn't take long to reach its destination. And when it did, its intended victim was gone. Only the softly glowing embers of the dying campfire remained. The scent of the big man the she-bat would have destroyed.

* * *

Kill them; kill them all. I should have. They were Seerco's final thoughts as the night gave way to dawn. Seerco had been lost in those thoughts as the night slipped away. A dim red litten dawn was slowly creeping across desolate eastern Celotia. The bloated red sun hung just below the horizon. The dusty atmosphere was beginning to clear just as Seerco's thoughts were beginning to clear. Yes, the night had slipped away. So had Nalia, he suddenly realized.

A sudden uneasy feeling overcame Seerco. He had let his guard down. And his past caught up with him.

"Seerco!"

The voice was quick. Jabbing and lethal. Like a poisoned *taunga* dart. Seerco knew it well. And knew it was only a matter of time. He jumped to his feet and turned. No irony; they hadn't made it to Chaon Gacca. But it would make no difference.

Senedgian stood across a windswept open space dotted with short jagged pinnacles like teeth jutting out of the ground. The great broadsword was held high, free hand a clinched fist, and a barely perceptible smile that spread to a sneering grin.

"It has been a long time, Senedgian," Seerco was calm.

Senedgian glared. "You ready die, Seerco?" he bellowed, and started a slow steady walk toward Seerco.

"I shall see you dead, Senedgian," Seerco growled.

Senedgian arched his eyebrow. "Dead? Dead?" he roared with laughter. "Like Kaasher dead? Like Gallen dead?" A pause then,

"Like Glys and Tarbo dead when you sent to kill wanderers. You betray Senedgian, kill Glys and Tarbo, wanderers go away safe. Senedgian don't forgive."

"They were an innocent family...," Seerco began.

"Innocent?" Senedgian interrupted. "Not like you, Seerco! You kill Nailok too?"

"I didn't kill Gallen, Kaasher, or Nailok," Seerco replied.

"You kill; that your way, assassin; I teach you!" Senedgian shouted. He tossed his sword aside, and growled, "I no need sword. I kill you with bare hands."

"I killed them." It was Nalia. She appeared from behind a jagged boulder a short distance behind Seerco.

Time stopped. Seerco turned. A mistake.

The big man slowed then stopped; there was a glaring fire in his one good eye that was locked on the tall lithe figure. "You?" he burst out in laughter. "You kill Kaasher, Gallen?"

"And the other," she nodded with a smile.

"Who you?" Senedgian's laughter ceased; his voice turned soft, but menacing. He took a step forward.

"Queen Lunalia of Tasuun," came the response.

"I hear stories – witch, vampire, Famorgh's woman," Senedgian said. He paused; his grin widened as his eye suddenly shifted to the unwary Seerco. "Soon be Senedgian's woman," he added and lunged at Seerco. The big man pulled the dagger from his boot and buried it deep into Seerco just under the ribs. The blade ripped upward, insuring a cut of death.

Surprised by Senedgian's agility and his own fatal mistake, Seerco pushed off the big man and stumbled backward. He doubled over, hands grasping the wound, and collapsed to the ground.

Senedgian laughed a howling laughter of triumph, but only for a moment. Lunalia launched at the big man, transforming in flight. Senedgian turned, looked up, and saw the towering she-bat baring down on him. He barely had time to raise both arms as claws and gnashing teeth tore into him. The big man howled in pain and agony as the she-bat's wings beat furious around them while Lunalia ripped an arm from its socket and tossed it aside before ripping Senedgian's head from his shoulders, and a snap snap snap of cracking ribs as the big man's spinal column was ripped out of his back with his head, beads of blood and bits of flesh arcing high into the air.

Seerca's eyes were clouding. He looked up, a slow arc of blood and pieces of flesh crossing his field of vision. Suddenly everything was quiet, a silence that lingered only momentarily. The pain went away, and Seerco's world softened, became serene, ethereal. He coughed. A trickle of blood appeared at the corner of his mouth. Eyes squinted to force back pain. Blood choked him. He coughed again, gasped for air then settled.

Queen Lunalia was at his side. She sat next to the dying killer, cradled his head in her arms. He looked up, coughed, and smiled.

"A fitting end for an assassin," Seerco said, a slow chuckling smile of irony appearing. A breath caught in his throat. He turned his eyes to the sky, paused then slowly closed them. He was fading.

Lunalia knew she could bring him back. But there was only one way. She bared her fangs, tilted Seerco's head, and paused. *I must,* her mind screamed. It was his only chance to live. At least live as she had lived for centuries. Strange her feelings for this man that she couldn't explain.

"The dying shall die," echoed a voice all around her.

Lunalia looked up, peered about. No one was there. But the voice was real. A female voice that was soft and soothing, yet powerful.

"Who are you that..."

"The dying shall die," the voice repeated. "In the end, only I shall remain."

A lone tear, long in coming, rolled down Queen Lunalia's cheek. Dal Seerco died.

*   *   *

There she stood, beyond the flames of Seerco's funeral pyre. She was the one who had spoken. Young to the eye, beautiful and dignified, Lunalia knew that this mysterious woman was far more ancient than she. The woman smiled as she noted Lunalia's attention. In the blink of an eye, she stood face to face with the last Queen of Tasuun. A spell was cast. Lunalia was captivated. Her breath caught in her throat and her heart began to race. She could do nothing but stare into those magnificent ancient eyes.

The mysterious woman slowly circled Lunalia. Her fingertips brushed over Lunalia's lips, cheek, ear, hair until the mysterious woman stood behind the last Queen of Tasuun. She gently brushed Lunalia's hair aside, revealing the back of her neck. With a hissing snarl, she tore into the back of Lunalia's neck like a hissing snarling *gratchet* tearing into a fresh *taunga* kill, sucking out brain, blood, and spinal fluid.

Lunalia's body was wracked with orgasms as she sank to her knees. She gasped one last time as the light faded from her eyes and then died.

"Only I shall remain," the mysterious woman cackled as she released the lifeless body.

With the setting of the bloated red sun the last Queen of Tasuun would be carrion for the night creatures of Celotia.

The House of Tuluroch

1

Dimonog, the last King of Tasuun, was diseased, corrupt of flesh. But he was not an old man. He was a beaten man, destroyed by time, and greed, and hatred. He sat, waiting to die just as his kingdom had died. He had outlasted everyone in his kingdom. Everyone but she, the woman from another time. Another place. And the thief who had entered his palace and now paced the floor before him.

Footprints appeared in the dust. The thief's heels clicked on the tiled floor. Dimonog was slumped forward on his throne, his eyes slowly following the thief's path. *How dare this common thief...* The king's thoughts trailed away and wandered. He faded in and out of sanity, chuckling softly. The thief stopped and glanced at the king.

"You come to steal my kingdom, thief?" the king stammered.

"I'm not a thief," the man said with a slight bow. "I'm Strahd Zarok, adventurer."

Dimonog chuckled again as his eyes trailed across the room, his mind beginning to wander. The king shook his head and turned his eyes back to Zarok. "Strahd Zarok, adventurer," he muttered, his thoughts repeating the man's claim. "Well, Strahd Zarok, adventurer, there's no kingdom left to steal. All gone. All gone." He muttered under his breath. "Only I survive. A king without a kingdom. A king without subjects."

"There are few left in all Zothique," Zarok replied.

"Tell me, adventurer," Dimonog said, ignoring Zarok's comment, "what are you doing in my palace if not here to thieve?"

Zarok grinned. "Just passing through."

"To where?"

"To wherever the road leads where I may find others."

"You may find none," Dimonog said as he shifted on his throne. "You've just said there are few left in all Zothique. I can tell you that there's no one to the south all the way to the sea. The land is barren, desolate. You shall find only death there."

"I know, I've just come north from Zhel..."

"To the east is a small enclave...," Dimonog muttered. His eyes were wide, his voice soft while speaking his wandering thoughts until they fell silent. He was blindly staring, seeing something else. Somewhere else. "The House of Tuluroch," Dimonog finally added.

"The what?" Zarok took a step closer.

The king glanced at Zarok. "House of Tuluroch."

"There are people there?"

"A few."

Zarok paused. Puzzled. *How should this man...* "How do you know this?" Zarok questioned.

King Dimonog raised a hand to the side of his neck and tilted his head slightly. "I have my ways," he answered.

Sure you do. The King of Tasuun looked like he hardly knew where he was let alone anyone else on the entire continent. But Zarok shrugged it off.

"So tell me, where might I find this House of Tuluroch?"

"In southeast...Ustaim," the king said. "On the coast of the Orient Sea." His eyes turned vacant and staring, his mind wandering again. "Yes...yes...the Orient Sea," he muttered in a soft dreamy voice.

Zarok smiled. "Well, now, you enjoy your kingdom." He turned and started away.

"My kingdom, yes...yes...," his voice trailed away as his eyes began to trace the dust on the floor.

"Oh, one more thing, mighty King Dimonog," Zarok chuckled in derision. He stopped and turned to the king a final time. "I was a thief, but with so few left, what is a thief? I can take what I want.

And you, mighty king...," He paused, his eyes gleaming, his smile widening. "You have nothing I want!"

His laughter echoed through the ruined hall as he turned and walked away. The clicking of his heels on the fractured marble floor and his laughter soon faded. Then he was gone. Silence fell upon the ruined palace of King Dimonog.

An apparition suddenly appeared in the king's thoughts. "Lilith!" Dimonog forced a shout. He was rubbing the side of his neck. There was a wound, two puncture marks that Zarok had failed to notice. "Lilith! Where are you?"

The tall lithe woman in filmy gown, milky white skin, and long black hair stepped from the shadows behind the throne. She was young, but timeless. "I'm here, little king," she said with a wry grin.

Dimonog struggled to turn, looking back over his shoulder.

"A king without a kingdom," Lilith said softly, her eyes distant. She slowly ran her fingers over his shoulders then clutched his hair. "It is time for Tasuun to die."

Like some rabid beast, she bit into Dimonog's neck, tearing away chunks of flesh and muscle. Her teeth grated on neck vertebrae. She snarled, slipped her fingers into his neck wound, and tore his head form his body. Dimonog's headless body slumped to the floor. Lilith flipped the head over, buried her face into the gore of Dimonog's severed neck, and drank the still warm blood.

The last king was dead. The Kingdom of Tasuun was at an end.

2

The old man sat on a boulder by the side of the road. He was leaning over a book, shoulders hunched. It was an old book. Thick. Dusty. Wire bound. Strange hand written words and hand drawn symbols were on the pages. Withered and ancient fingers trailed the words across the page as the old man studied them. The page was near the end of the book. Only three more pages to go. At times he chuckled. At times he grunted. At times wrinkled fingers tapped the pages. He was apparently delighted.

Then there was a sound. The old man paused, staring at the dusty narrow dirt road before him. He mumbled under his breath. Someone was coming. On the road. It didn't surprise him. Even with the few who remained in all Zothique, it didn't surprise him. In fact, he knew the man would approach. He had known it for quite some time. So, he closed the book, stuffed it between two boulders behind him, and grinned as he watched the beast and its rider approach.

Just an old man sitting there, Zarok saw as he approached on the back of his dromedary. The one time thief smiled as he studied the man seated on the boulder. The man was small, frail; with long thin white hair. Bald on top. His clothing were but tattered rags. Sandals were upon his feet. He was weather worn, perhaps not long for this world. But these days, no one was long for the world. One thing Zarok did notice as he reined his dromedary to a stop was the man's eyes. They were bright and attentive. The old man had his wits. More than could be said for King Dimonog.

"Hello old man," Zarok said in as friendly a voice as he could.

"Scye," Scye replied. "'Name's Scye. And hello there yerself, young fella."

He held out a hand. Zarok took it.

"Strahd Zarok, adventurer."

"Sit yerself down here on a rock," Scye said with a gesture. He chuckled as he added, "Had lotta adventures, have ya?"

Zarok sat himself down. Hands on his knees, he leaned forward and looked over at Scye. "Yes, have a few adventures now and then. Most every day is an adventure now. Just staying alive."

"Didn't 'spect to see anyone here 'bouts," Scye lied. He smiled, his eyes squinting. "Least ways on this road. You headin' someplace for more adventure?"

Zarok nodded. "Yes, you might say that."

"Now where might that be?"

"East to the House of Tuluroch."

"Ya wouldn't be speakin' of the Ustaim Tuluroch's?"

Zarok nodded again. "The very same."

"Well now."

"King Dimonog told me..."

"Dimonog?" Scye interrupted. "He lives? He's a silly one."

"You been to the House of Tuluroch?" Zarok said, ignoring the old man's rant about the Tasuun king.

"Been there a time or two," Scye answered. He suddenly gestured with a swing of a hand. "They's out thata away. 'Bout a day's travel. Can't miss it. Ya just stays right here on this road yur on, and it'll take you right up to their gate. Big wooden gate it is. Two doors."

"Walled?"

"Yeah, on three sides. Fourth side fell into the ocean. The place is perched on a cliff and it's crumblin'." Scye paused, winked at Zarok, and chuckled. "The cliffs, and the rest of the walls. That's what's crumblin'. The house ain't much better. Old and fallin' apart. Like the rest of Zothique."

Zarok laughed. "You like to talk, don't you, old man?"

"I talk when there's something to say," Scye replied. Without missing a beat, he continued, "There was this astrologer, Nushain was his name; he wasn't a very good astrologer. He saw three new stars in the heavens and thought it some sign that would lead him..."

"Old man, old man!" Zarok interrupted with a laugh. He gestured with a hand and shook his head. "I need not your story of some astrologer."

As Zarok's laughter faded away, there was a soft distant sighing of wind in the air. The former thief peered about. Scye glanced at him and smiled.

"If ya travel to Tuluroch, ya best be on your way," Scye softly. "The sun's gonna go down soon and there's thing's in the dark..."

"Nothing lives," Zarok interrupted. "The Ghorii are gone, and no wizards and sorcerers to conjure demons." He paused, chuckled. "And no thieves on this road."

"There are djinns that conjure themselves. I seen 'em."

Zarok stared at Scye then slowly rose to his feet. "Yes, I suppose its best that I be on my way."

Scye jumped from the boulder as Zarok mounted his dromedary. "Think I could catch a ride with ya there, young fella?"

Zarok reached down with a hand. "You just climb on up here old man. And hold on."

"Scye," the old man grunted as Zarok wrenched him up and he slipped into place behind the former thief.

"Old man," Zarok replied, and burst into laughter as the two of them started down the road toward the House of Tuluroch.

Seated behind the former thief, the old man was smiling.

* * *

The bloated red sun had set. The orange sky was depending. The clawing shadows from sparse vegetation spread, growing longer, digging at the patched landscape. A black shadow suddenly rose up near the stable behind the House of Tuluroch. Tendrils of blackness writhed from a towering column of black. It moved slowly, silently, arcing over the stable.

Inside, two stabled dromedaries bayed nervously. They bucked and shuffled about in their stalls. Crog, the stable boy, looked up. He glanced toward the two beasts in their stalls then peered about, wide eyed. It had grown perceptibly cold in the stable, much too cold for this time of year. Then the stable began to disappear, seeming to fade into black as a shadow pushed through the walls from outside, entering through cracks and gaps between the wooden slats. It reformed into a pulsing mass, a great towering column that reared up from the floor and over Crog's head.

Crog stumbled back. The air became frigid. The light of torches suddenly vanished. Crog gasped for air while shielding his eyes from a blazing glare of blackness. He wanted to scream. Writhing tendrils of black reached for him. The black shadow enfolded him.

* * *

The aging warrior, Sarokhan Tuluroch, was crossing the compound, returning to the house. He had just barred and locked the gates for the night. Certain there would be no trouble, it was best to lock them anyway. Should any scavengers arrive unexpectedly and get inside the compound... Unthinkable. Tuluroch knew there were few left in all of Zothique, but he wasn't taking chances. At least for the sake of his daughters, Eclin and Esherel, and their friend, Alea Garanase.

Of course, the gates would be no barrier to the djinn. But they never bothered the Tuluroch family. As far as Sarokhan Tuluroch knew the djinn had never bothered the family. Some said djinns came on a cold wind. That troubled Tuluroch. Five of his household had disappeared without a trace. There had been a brief coldness in the air each time. Just like the brief coldness Tuluroch had felt as he locked the gate. He knew without having to be told that another of his household had disappeared. He knew that no one saw or heard.

"Sarokhan," came a voice.

The aging warrior stopped and turned. The voice was Sokol Sool, one of the two remaining guards that watched over the Tuluroch compound during the night. Sool and Vilo Sinjar were crossing the compound to take up their posts in the corner guard towers.

"I know," Tuluroch said. His voice was soft, weary. "I felt the cold. Who was it this time?"

The two guards joined him. "It was Crog," Sinjar said softly. "Gone without a trace."

Tuluroch sighed. "The stable boy. Alright, well, keep an eye open." The aging warrior brushed past, headed for the house.

Sinjar and Sool watched him leave before parting for their prospective guard towers.

* * *

The campfire flame flickered. Embers rode a current of hot air into the cooling night sky. Zarok watched the flames dance in the eyes of the old man. Those eyes were unsettling. Clear and deep. Wise. This old man had been around. Had seen the world. Knew more than Zarok would ever hope to know. The former thief was well aware of it. There was something captivating about the old man. True that he presented a comical figure by his speech and his appearance. But those eyes. Those intense piercing eyes belayed a buffoon.

But the old man knew things. Or picked up on things that Zarok was completely unaware of. Like a djinn being nearby. That had caught Zarok by surprise. How the old man could know. But Zarok didn't doubt him a bit. It was in his eyes as he looked up from the fire, a smile crawling across his face. He stared at Zarok.

"It's out there," the Scye had said softly.

"What's out there?" Zarok had questioned.

"The djinn."

118

A sudden cackling in the dark echoed softly across the camp. The campfire fluttered as though caught in a faint breeze. A black form shifted against the stars, a silhouette of some…thing. It danced in the night, shimmering on a soft wind, sounding like a fluttering sail of an ancient galley plying the waters of the Indaskian Sea. Then it was gone. There was silence but for the crackling flame of the campfire.

"It was a djinn," Zarok said timidly. Almost a whisper.

"Yeah yeah, a djinn," Scye chuckled. "Come to see us. Maybe now goin' to see the Tuluroch's. Whisk away one of them purty girls that's there." The old man's smile widened. The comment had been a tease. He waited for a reaction, but didn't get one. Zarok knew it for what it was.

"As long as it doesn't come back here," Zarok said softly, his eyes plying the night.

3

"Nothing," Sinjar said. "The night was quiet."

Sool nodded agreement. The guards were standing with Sarokhan in front of the house near the gate. The sun was newly risen, the air already hot and hazy.

"We've lasted another night without interruption," Sarokhan said with a sigh.

"Sir, I, well…," Sinjar began. Uncertain, his words trailed off.

"Yes, speak your mind," Sarokhan said. His eyes narrowed.

"There were faint voices and laughter carried on the night wind," Sinjar said. "Far off and only a short time."

Sarokhan nodded. "Djinn."

"Yes, if any remain, I think…," Sinjar was saying.

"Father!"

The three men turned. Sarokhan's youngest daughter, Esherel, was running from the house in her nightgown. Behind her, on the porch, stood the young lady adventurer, Alea Garanase.

"Manadara's gone!" Esherel exclaimed. She stopped, gasping to catch her breath.

Her father, silent, laid a hand on her shoulder. The two guards exchanged glances while Garanase stared at the snow covered peak of Sha-kag in the distance.

"I want everyone in the...," Sarokhan began.

A hard knock on the gate interrupted him.

"Hey! Anyone in there!" came a strange voice, a human voice.

Sinjar and Sool ran for their towers.

"Well, you going to open this gate?" Strahd Zarok called out. He was indignant, a little short tempered. It was the heat.

"Just a traveler on a dromedary," Sool called out to Sarokhan.

The old man's head suddenly popped up over Zarok's shoulder. "Sool!" he bellowed. "Open the gate 'fore I call a Mordiggian curse on ya!"

Sool laughed as he peered down at the old man. "And old Scye too," he called out to Sarokhan.

Sool and Sinjar hurried down from the towers as Sarokhan swung the gate open. Zarok and Scye passed through on the dromedary and reined it to a stop as the three men and two women gathered around.

"What brought you back here, old man?" Sarokhan questioned.

"He did!" Scye replied as Zarok helped the old man to the ground then climbed down himself.

"Strahd Zarok." He offered a hand. Sarokhan took it.

"Didn't know there was anyone left here abouts," Sarokhan said. "Not sure if it's the wisest thing to come here."

"Cliff wall still crumblin out back?" Scye questioned.

"Still is," Sarakhan said with a nod, "but that's not the problem."

Scye tilted his head and planted his hands on his hips. "Well, now, just what IS the problem?"

Sarokhan paused, staring at the old man. "I'll tell you inside," he finally said. Turning to Garanase, he added, "Stable Mister Zarok's beast then meet us in the great room."

Garanase nodded, took the reins and led the dromedary away.

"Come inside," Sarokhan said. He turned toward the house.

* * *

"A friend of Scye's is a friend of the Tulurochs," Sarokhan was saying to Zarok.

"Let's not git all gushy with feelins," Scye grunted. "Tell us what's happenin' here."

Sarohkan sighed, paced around one end of a long feasting table and stopped. "Peope've have been disappearing," he said softly.

"Huh!" Scye chuckled. "Yur kiddin'. People been disappearin' for a long time."

"You're talking about Zothique, Scye," Sarokhan replied. "I'm talking about here, the House of Tuluroch. Our people have been disappearing." Sarokhan paused. His eyes shifted, glancing at those gathered. "My daughters, Eclin and Esherel, Sokkol Sool, Vilo Sinjar, Alea Garanase, myself. We're all that's left in this house. We lost the stable boy last night. And our house keeper, Manadara Jezz, this morning."

"Lost?" Zarok replied.

Sarokhan nodded. "Lost. Disappeared. Without a trace. None of us witnessed..."

"There IS a brief spell of cold air," Sinjar suddenly interrupted.

"Sounds like Mordiggian to me," Scye replied.

"Mordiggian?" Zarok questioned with a chuckle. "Nonsense."

"Maybe it's him," Alea Garanase suddenly said from the door. She had returned unnoticed.

"Who?" Sarokhan questioned.

"Sha-kag," she replied. "Maybe he's still alive."

Zarok's eyes darted, his head turned, seeking explanation. "Who is this Sha-kag?"

"An old sorcerer," Garanase replied. "Lives up on the mountain. Came from the Isle of Naat centuries ago. Founded Sha-karag. At least so says the legend."

"Well then, maybe we should just go see what's there," Zarok said. He turned to Scye. "What do you say, old man?"

"Oh no, sonny," Scye replied with a shake of his head. "I'm much to old ta be climbin' mountains. Ya never know when the end is gonna come, and I wanna put it off 'slong as possible."

"Anyone?" Zarok challeneged.

"I'll go," Garanase replied. "Kinda curious."

Zarok turned to Sarokhan. "The lady and I'll go," he said. "Two of us can travel faster."

"If you find Sha-kag alive, you won't be coming back," Sarokhan warned.

"We'll be back," Zarok said. His eye contact held Sarokhan for a moment then turned to the door. Taping Garanase on the shoulder, he added, "Let's go."

The former thief and the lady adventurer left the house.

4

Alea Garanase knew the quickest route to the summit of Sha-kag's maountain. Still, it would take more than a day to get there. They'd have to spend the night out in the open, concealed as much as possible. The two moved as quick as they could. Garanase led the way through the rock strewn barren wasteland into the foothills. Through gulleys, narrow valleys, and dried river washes she jumped, hopped, skipped, stretching from boulder to boulder. Zarok took notice of her form as she stretched, balancing on the rocks and boulders. She knew it. He smiled.

"Don't get any ideas," she grumbled as she jumped rock to rock, Zarok close behind. Her tone wasn't so much threatening as it was a casual warning.

"I wonder," Zarok began, trying to keep up with her.

"You wonder what," Garanase said, a statement.

"I wonder you dressed as a man and wear a saber, yet you are a beautiful young woman..."

"The saber's for protection," Garanase interrupted. "And I dress to travel. I'm an adventurer, like you. Are you not?"

"Yes, yes," Zarok replied. He was winded, still trying to keep pace with her. "I have been an adventurer. Like you."

"Have been?"

"There aren't many adventures left," he replied. "Not many adventurers left."

It was true. No one knew how many people were left. Garanase remained silent.

"So tell me, young adventurer," Zarok continued. "You are not of the House of Tuluroch."

"No, I'm not," she replied. "I came there a winter's past. They took me in. I became friends with Esherel Tuluroch."

"Then what?"

Garanase stopped and turned. She laid a hand on her hip, the other hand on the hilt of her saber, and tilted her head. She was squinting, the bloated red setting sun in her eyes.

"What what?" she questioned. She was brusque, caring not for Zarok's questions.

"Then what?" Zarok repeated. "What are you if not of the House of Tuluroch?"

"That's my business," she replied then turned and kept going.

Zarok watched her for a moment, his eyes trailing her form, his smile widened. A feisty one, she was. And secretive. He chuckled. And followed after her again.

* * *

The day had come and gone quickly. Night had fallen by the time Zarok and Garanase had reached the base of the mountain. With the night came the cold. But they lit no fire for warmth. There were cries in the dark. Strange cries. A hideous howling noise. A fire would draw them. Creatures, some misshapen beasts. Hungry, searching for prey. Or djinns. Seeking to curse what was left of the people of Zothique. Zarok and Garanase didn't intend to be victims.

"I told you about me," Garanase whispered in the dark. "What about you?"

She couldn't see Zarok in the dark. But he was near. Two arm's length away. Sitting crouched, knees drawn up. Just like her.

"Shhhhhhhhhhhhhhhhh," came the whispered response. "You hear that? Be quiet."

The cries continued, but more feverish now. Closer. Crouching in the dark, crawling toward them. Whatever was making that noise, it was all around them. Then a sudden breeze whistled between boulders. It ruffled their hair, their clothing. It was a cold breeze. A night breeze, Zarok was certain. And when it had passed, the cries in the dark had fallen silent.

"They're gone," Garanase whispered.

"Or maybe they're just quiet," Zarok whispered a replied. "Like we should be. Get some sleep; we may have a fight on our hands tomorrow." He sat quietly listening. He heard Garanase stretch out on the ground then fall silent. The cries in the dark never returned that rest of the night.

* * *

A cold wind rose up. It raced across the barren wasteland toward the coast. Howling cries of death rode with the wind. And as it neared, a black shade, blacker than the night that shrouded the House of Tuluroch crept silently toward the compound. The shade flowed up and over the wall and into the compound like water over rocks. Sool stood in his guard tower, keeping watch on the night. He never saw the shade rise up and engulf the tower. And when the shade left the tower and crept toward the house, the tower was empty and silent.

5

The bloated red sun hung overhead. It was midday. The air was cold and biting. Zarok and Garanase had reached an ice shelf just below the summit of Sha-kag's mountain. There was a cave, an entrance to a cavern, a place to pause and rest. The two adventurers exchanged glances and then started toward the cavern entrance.

"I think Sha-kag lives in a cave," Garanase said as she drew her saber.

"Maybe this one," Zarok replied.

"It might be," Garanase said as they entered the cave.

It was. The underground cavern was a frozen ruin. A mist of ice crystals hung in the air. A sheet of ice glazed the floor, covering debris that lay scattered about. The cavern was softly aglow in an unearthly light.

"You think the light is sorcery?" Zarok questioned as the two of them slowly crossed the cavern.

"I would say no," Garanase replied. She was watching the figure on the throne. A great figure seated opposite the cavern entrance. It was dead, reduced to little more than a skeleton, a great skull with empty eye sockets hanging on its chest of bones.

"I guess it's not your sorcerer," Zarok said as they paused in the center of the cavern.

"I guess not," she agreed.

Suddenly, there was faint laughter. It came from afar. Not inside the cave, but from without. Through the cold frigid air. It was a cackling laughter, dark, maniacal. Then came a clattering of bones. Zarok and Garanase watched the skeleton shake on the throne then force itself to stand. It stumbled from the throne to the floor and danced as the two adventurers watched. They were captivated by a collection of bones from a long dead sorcerer cavorted across the floor, dancing madly, pirouetting in a mad semblance of court dancers before a great king the likes of which hadn't been seen in Zothique for centuries. Then suddenly the skeleton of Sha-kag stopped. It hovered for a moment, swaying back and forth then collapsed into a pile of bones in the middle of the cavern floor.

"Best we get back to the House of Tuluroch," Zarok said softly, his eyes on the bones of the dead sorcerer.

* * *

The bloated blood red sun was riding low in the evening sky, nearing the horizon. Three days gone, Zarok and Garanase had hoped to be back at the House of Tuluroch before nightfall. As they neared, they heard a calamity, a splitting of rock and earth, a splintering of wood. Dust and smoke billowed into the orange sky. It was coming from the direction of the Tuluroch compound.

"The cliff is taking the house!" Garanase cried. "It's crumbling!"

They ran. And didn't stop running until they met Vilo Sinjar on the narrow road leading from the gate. Sinjar was beaten, weathered, soiled clothing, and the marks of a battle scarred him.

"Don't go," he pleaded with Zarok and Garanase. His breath was short, hoarse. He gasped to speak again. "There's no one left. ...all gone. They're gone. Disappeared like the others."

"The cliff, we heard..." Garanase began.

"Not the cliff," Sinjar interrupted. He shook his head. "The house destroyed. There was a shadow. And a cold wind...cold cold wind."

"Mordiggian," Zarok whispered reverently. "The old man was right after all."

"I've got to see." Garanase brushed past Sinjar. Zarok followed.

Sinjar turned on the road and watched as the two adventurers rounded the corner and disappeared. Then he smiled. "Mordiggian," he voiced his thoughts softly with a grin. "Yes, Mordiggian." And a soft cold wind blew with him as he turned and continued down the road until he faded into a soft shade and then the shade disappeared.

*　*　*

The house lay in ruins. The place abandoned, looked as though it had been abandoned winters past. No one would know the story here. No one knew the truth save one. Perhaps two. Zarok shook his head as he peered about the compound. He was mounted on his dromedary, ready to leave. Holding the reins was Alea Garanase. She looked up at the former thief turned former adventurer. He looked down at her, smiled, and took the reins.

"You sure you don't want to come with me?" he questioned.

"Yeah, I've my own path to follow," she replied.

"Follow to where?" Zarok questioned.

"I don't know," she replied. "To the end of Zothique, I suppose."

Zarok shifted in the saddle and pulled on the reins. "Alright," he said. "Fare travels then, Alea Garanase."

She nodded.

Zarok shook the reins and the dromedary cantered through the gate and out of the Tuluroch compound. Garanase watched as the dromedary carried the former thief further and further down the road. Dust obscured the beast and the man. For a moment, she regretted not going with him, but quickly dismissed the thought. She sighed and looked up. The orange sky was darkening. The days of Zothique were darkening.

"To the end of Zothique." The voice was soft, female, alluring and musical.

Garanase turned. A woman stood near the porch of the ruined House of Tuluroch. She was tall, beautiful, with long black hair and milk white skin. The wisdom of ages shown in her eyes.

"I can take you there," she said with a smile. "To the end of Zothique."

She raised a hand and held it out to Garanase. Slowly, the young adventurer crossed the compound and took Lilith's hand.

* * *

The old man sat on the boulder, the ancient tome spread open in his lap. He was near the end of the book. There had been three blank pages, now only two remained. He stared at the figures that had appeared. New figures, figures of the newly dead, figures of destiny. He chuckled. It had been a glorious few days. He sighed, satisfied then chuckled again as a thought crossed his mind. Only a few days remained. The old man turned the page. The next page was empty. So was the last. But soon they would both be filled and the book would be complete. The Age of Zothique would be over.

Night Shades of Ilcar

1

The eyes of the old peasant Tarkald darted fearfully back and forth between the western horizon and the road ahead. The sun was setting. He still had a long way to go to get back to the tavern ruins near the village of Silomme. Searching for food had taken him further a field this time. He had lost track of distance. And time. He hadn't watched the bloated red sun slipping in the western sky. Night would come quick here in the north of Zothique. Old Tarkald had to get back to the tavern.

There was a placed along the road to Silomme. Those old stone ruins. They couldn't be avoided. There was a time when Tarkald wouldn't care. But a fortnight ago, something had come to those ruins. Whatever it was, it was evil. There were signs. Strange lights. The clouds. The thunder and no rain. Soft whispering voices. They sounded like sirens. At first Tarkald thought it might be djinns. But then he saw the black haired woman walking in the ruins in the light of day. No no, not djinns, he was now convinced. Something else.

Tarkald shook the reins to quicken the pace. The two oxen pulling the old wagon lumbered forward slightly faster. It would be dark soon. Too soon. Strange things would begin. Tarkald had to get past the ruins, had to get back to Silomme. He swallowed hard, his mind focused on the stone ruins. Around the bend and there they were, dark and ominous, set back from the road in a blasted, barren wasteland. The red sun had set. The sky was a darkening to orange. Shadows were beginning to crawl through those ancient ruins.

Tarkald suddenly pulled up on the reins. The oxen stopped in the middle of the road. They snorted nervously, shuffling hooves. Tarkald took his eyes from the ruins and peered down the road. A dark demonic vision was looming toward him on the narrow road. It was a dark thing on a black dromedary, riding hard. Tarkald's eyes went wide as he watched the rapidly approaching demon, its black dromedary breathing fire. A cloud of dust fanned out behind the demon rider and beast.

"It's the day of my death," Tarkald whispered, the demon rider drawing closer.

The demon rider suddenly drew up alongside Tarkald. The old peasant peered up at the rider and his imagination settled, his mind cleared. It had been the imaginative power of the stone ruins that had clouded his judgment. This was no demon, no fire breathing dromedary. Tarkald let out a sigh of relief.

"I'm Koranni Fakoud," the man said. He was a big man. Strong, black of skin, a southern desert nomad attired in nomadic balloon trousers and an ornately embroidered vest. "You ride to Silomme?"

"Near enough," Tarkald replied, rapidly shaking his head in acknowledgment. "I go home. I must go soon. Before dark."

"Before dark?" Fakoud questioned.

Tarkald nodded. "Before dark," he said fearfully, still shaking his head. "Bad things happen. Strange things. A fortnight gone, ever since something come to the ruins..."

"Ruins?" Fakoud interrupted.

Tarkald pointed. "There," he said, voice squeaking with fear. "There; you see them. I go! Before dark!"

The old peasant shook the reins and his oxen lurched forward. Fakoud's dromedary danced back off the edge of the road. The desert nomad shook his head, reined his dromedary around the way he'd come, and watched the old peasant disappear down the road. Fakoud grinned. *Old peasants and their superstitions,* he thought.

He turned his eyes to the stone ruins. Only a short distance off the road. One could walk to them. Fakoud was curious. The old peasant had been terrified. The sky was growing darker, the shadows longer. The ruins looked like a great beast lying upon the land. Fakoud was captivated. He reined his dromedary around and started toward them.

Half way he stopped, dismounted and continued on foot. Amidst the stones, the broken walls, the open window frames and doorways, a mist began to rise. On the wind, Fakoud thought he heard a soft voice, a whisper, drawing him ever closer to the ruins.

* * *

Over the past fortnight Naras Naran had grown more cautious. She stayed hidden more often. Crouched in dark corners of the decayed tavern, under tables, in closets. She knew about the ruins out on the old Silomme Road. Something was there. Something evil. She had had a connection with it. Tarkald knew she had had a connection. He had noticed when it first happened. A fortnight ago. Her mood had changed. Naran had become fearful. She wasn't the same Naras Naran that Tarkald had taken under his wing to protect her though she needed no protection at the time. There had been no one to protect her from. Still, Tarkald felt it his duty. After all, she was young and a deaf mute. And now she had a connection to some thing that lurked amidst the old stone ruins out on the old Silomme Road.

The sun had long set. Naran hurried through the side streets and alleys of Silomme. No one was about. There hadn't been in years. Silomme was a dead city with Tarkald and Naran its only inhabitant. But out on the old Silomme Road, in the old stone ruins…something had come. Naran had to get back to the tavern. Old Tarkald would be coming back with food. They wouldd be safe. The two of them. From whatever had come out of the night. That thing, it was watching. From above. Naran knew it. She felt it. It had been in Silomme before, skirting the ruined rooftops. And it was there now. Somewhere up there in the gathering shadows. It was following Naran. Closer. Closer.

Naran tried to cry out, but couldn't. Her eyes were wild. She ran as fast as she could. Ran for her life. Jumping and skipping around trash and debris that littered the alleys and side streets. Then tripped and fell. Sprawled against the crumbling pavement. *It's gonna get me,* her thoughts screamed silently. *It's gonna…* It didn't. It was gone. The thing that was so near had suddenly vanished. Something had distracted it. Naran breathed a sigh of relief.

The shadows were long and growing longer. The sky had long since faded to a deep crimson and was now darkening to black. Hands on hips, Fakoud stood at the ruins. His eyes held them tight, surveying them in the quickly fading dusk. The ruins had aged beyond their destruction. Many blocks, boulders, and stones were overgrown with moss. Ages of wind had softened sharp edges and stripped the topsoil. There were legends about this place, legends Fakoud never knew. With the coming death of Zothique, he never would know.

Fakoud slowly strolled amidst the crumbling stone. The night crept in. Suddenly there was a feeling, a presence. Fakoud stopped, peered about, his eyes wide. There was nothing. Just silence and the dark. He continued, slowly, stepping around fallen rock. A shadow detached and followed him about the ruins. The feelings returned, an uneasiness and rising terror. The desert nomad felt them, but also knew them to be real, tangible, lurking amidst the fallen stones. Fakoud stopped. He held his breath as he slowly peered about. A short distance away his dromedary began to bay mournfully.

Amidst the ruins a vampire wraith walked and watched. The magnificent dark pools that were her eyes sparkled in the dark. It was a sparkle that Fakoud couldn't see. She smiled. Alluring. Seductive. But she was invisible to the desert nomad. She had made it so. She delighted in shadowing his every step, knowing he could not see her. Perhaps she would make this tall black skinned desert nomad her own. Her smile widened as she entertained the idea. A sudden thought struck her. *Lilith.* She would disapprove. All things, human and animal, belonged to her. There were so few left.

2

The night had come. The dark settled over the ruins of Silomme. The village was long dead, cries of the destitute long silent. The raging fires long extinguished. Only the ravages of time remained a threat to Silomme. Tarkald and Naras Naran were the only inhabitants that remained. Except when the Night Shades came. That's what Naran called them. Night Shades.

Tarkald climbed down from the wagon and stood in the dusty street. He listened. There was nothing. He peered into the inky blackness and could see nothing. He opened his senses to the night and was relieved. There were no feelings of fear or terror, feelings the old peasant felt when the Night Shades were near. Naran felt them more acutely. She could tell when they were coming. This night the Night Shades were apparently elsewhere.

In the dark the old peasant made his way to the ruined tavern that he shared with Naran. They called the place home. At least for now. Until the Night Shades found them there. Then they'd have to find another place to hide. If they could. Tarkald stopped on the wooden porch. He sighed, remembering days when the tavern was alive as Silomme had been alive. Those days were long gone now. But the memories were warm. They lingered. Tarkald smiled.

But the village and tavern were dead. Only their ghosts remained. The ghost of the tavern haunted Tarkald. He remembered the raucous laughter, the loud jeering propositions to the serving wenches, the fights erupting over games of chance, the slamming of empty tankards on table tops and the bar.

Then a shadow had crawled across the village, grasping villagers, buildings, and beasts alike. Decay gripped the village and Tarkald had fled. Slowly the village died. Abandoned to time, Silomme remained undisturbed until Tarkald returned to find Naras Naran. Tarkald wasn't even sure if that was her real name. But that's what he called her. That's what she muttered unintelligibly when he had caught her trying to steel his pack, not knowing anyone was till left in Silomme, much less left alive. She had stayed with him. Then the Night Shades came. He became her protector.

"Oughta just leave," Tarkald muttered the thought. He sighed as he entered the tavern. Inside the tavern, he stopped. It was dark. And quiet. Tarkald's eyes adjusted. He peered about the ruins, scanned the corners, searching for Naran. "Naras?" he called out softly.

There came the faintest of sounds from a dark corner. Tarkald smiled. He slowly crossed the tavern to the darkened corner. Naran gazed up at him from behind an overturned table. The old peasant noted the uncertainty in her eyes. He crouched on the floor next to the young woman, took her in his arms, and rocked her gently.

Soothing her fears. Naran was feeble minded, and losing her wits. Sometimes the old peasant wondered which would go first. Naran's mind or Zothique. He always came to the same conclusion. Naran's mind was far more gone than Zothique.

"I gotta do something," the old peasant said softly. "Look this here evil in the eye and kill it."

* * *

"Alea!" came the banshee-like angry howling wail amidst gnashing and grinding teeth.

A second later there was an explosion of thunder and lightning, and a howling demon wind. Lilith was there, suddenly, floating on the wind, hovering before Garanase. The ancient vampire's blue gown shimmered. Her long black hair arced on the wind like a wave. The vampire wraith hardly had time to gasp before Lilith's fingers were wrapped around her throat. Long claw-like nails punctured Garanase's milky white skin. Trails of thin crimson blood trickled down her neck. The breath of death was pungent in the night air. There was a fire blazing in Lilith's ancient eyes as they bore deep into the youthful vampire wraith. All about thunder, lightning, and howling of the mad demon wind continued.

"I made you what you are!" Lilith snarled while thunder crashed around her. "You belong to me. All things belong to me! That includes the black man! How dare you take it upon yourself for even a moment to think you can take what you want! I give to you what I think you deserve! You get nothing more!"

Lilith reared up above the ruins, dragging Garanase with her into the air. In a flash of lightning and crashing thunder, she sent the young vampire crashing to the barren wasteland beyond the ruins. Terrified, Garanase kept her distance. It was the first time in the one winter since the ancient vampire had taken Garanase from the ruins of Tuluroch that she had seen such hatred and disdain in Lilith's eyes. Lilith was a mysterious one. Garanase had learned only those things that Lilith allowed her to know. In the time they had spent together, roaming the barren parched landscape of a dying Zothique, scavenging the meager amounts of animals that remained for them to feed upon, Lilith had told Garanase little about herself. Only that she had been the first and would be the last. Whatever that meant. Garanase wasn't going to press it. She hadn't.

* * *

Like a ripple in the night air, that's what it felt like to Fakoud. A brief breeze he felt and then it was gone. Silence pervaded the stone ruins. He stopped and peered about. Nothing but the dark of night and darker forms of ruined walls. Still, something had happened. Fakoud didn't know what, but something had.

Then a voice, a soft whisper pervaded the night air. It trailed through the shadowed stone ruins. The whispering voice wove a melody through the dark, reflected off crumbling walls, turning corners. It was a voice of seduction and lust. A siren's voice. The voice rolled through the shadows on a current of air, softly plying through the still of the night.

Fakoud followed the soft whisper to its source. He rounded the corner of a ruined wall and stopped. She stood there. Tall, lithe, clothed in a soft light blue gown. Her skin was white and seemed to glow faintly. Her hair was long and black, and fell in waves about her shoulders. Her grin was that of a seductress. She hooked Fakoud. They approached, stood face to face. Her fingers trailed lightly over his cheek, and he was lost in her.

Here in the ruins of a far gone time. Here in the night beyond the ruins of a long dead village. Here stood a woman. Her deep eyes sparkled in the night and shown with wisdom of ages past. She had a power, a will, a strength unnatural that she exuded and Fakoud succumbed to. The tall black skinned desert nomad closed his eyes and reveled in her closeness as she leaned forward, fangs extending. There was a prick of skin. Fakoud gasped. Lilith drank deeply, holding Fakoud up as his knees began to buckle. Then she leaned close to an ear.

"Sleep," Lilith said as she gently lowered her prize to the ground.

Yes, sleep...and dream, an angered Garanase thought as she watched from the darkness. *I'll be there.*

Smoke and heat roared up the great staircase. The ornate stair covering and tapestries in the great entrance hall erupted in flame. The fire was spreading quickly. It fed on the oak furniture and huge tapestries that adorned the halls and rooms of the great chateau. Burning paneling, tapestry, and great wooden beams fell away. Fakoud struggled, wielding his scimitar to cut a path through the smoldering and burning destruction.

Hands blistered and burned, the desert nomad winced in pain while hacking his way through the entrance hall to the foot of the stairs. There he paused as fire roared up the staircase to the second floor. It was an impenetrable wall of flame. But Fakoud had to get through it; he must. He didn't know why. And turning his eyes to the top of the stairs, he saw a young woman on the landing just beyond the fire. The firelight danced on her face, and a name formed on Fakoud's lips.

"Alea," he whispered the name. "Alea Garanase."

He didn't know the woman nor the name. Nor did he know why the name had come to him. But he knew that the young woman on the landing was this same Alea Garanase. She smiled as she raised her hands and beckoned him to come to her.

Fakoud started up the stairs, hacking his way through the burning debris and flames. The fire licked his clothing, singed his hair, his skin, dried his eyes until they hurt. He gained the top of the stairs and turned toward Garanase. She walked untouched through the fire, smiled at Fakoud, and wrapped her arms around his neck. The desert nomad stared into those eyes as flames engulfed them. But it wasn't the beautiful young woman he saw. It was a beast, a thing of evil intent on feasting upon his blood and soul.

The beast transformed. It reared back and howled; its eyes a smoldering fire. Long jagged fangs dripped an oozing slime. There was a sudden explosion of smoke and flame beneath them. It roared up and obscured Fakoud's view of the beast. Only for a moment. When he could see the thing again, Fakoud found himself staring into the eyes of the black haired woman. She was smiling. The smile widened. She began to cackle.

Fakoud closed his eyes tight and then opened them again. The fire was gone. The chateau was in ruins as it had been for centuries. And Fakoud found himself sitting up naked on the dusty parched landscape, his clothing scattered about. A thin line of orange ran along the eastern horizon. Dawn was coming.

Jumping to his feet, Fakoud climbed into his clothes and brushed sand and soil from the sleeves of his garment. He turned his eyes to the stone ruins and saw a faint trace of charring on those ancient stones. Some time, long ago, there had been a fire there. In some forgotten time. Suddenly his dromedary bayed. Fakoud turned, saw the beast a short distance away kicking nervously at the parched ground, fearful of something unseen.

"Yes, you're right, best we leave, old friend," the desert nomad said. And he hurried to where his dromedary nervously waited.

3

Tarkald sat on the wooden bench seat of the buckboard wagon, reins in his hands. Naran was pleading with the old peasant. Not vocally, but in her expression. The look in her eyes. The mumbled sounds she made. She didn't want the old man to go. Something would happen, she knew it. What she didn't know was to whom it would happen. Tarkald or herself.

"Now now Naras," the old man was coxing, "you just stay hidden. I'll be back 'fore nightfall."

Naran shook her head violently.

"Now I got to git us some food," Tarkald tried to explain. "I didn't git none yesterday. We're gonna starve if'n…"

Naran pounded on the side of the wagon with a closed fist.

"Now now Naras," Tarkald continued, "you just go on back in the tavern; play that word game in your head. You can do it, I know you can."

She shook her head again. Tears were forming.

"I got to go," Tarkald said. His voice was edgy, impatient. "I can't stay here all day. 'Fore long the day'll be passed by. Now you do what I tells you." He shook the reins. The two oxen stepped forward. The wagon lurched.

Naran stepped back. She stood and watched as Tarkald moved on down the dusty barren street, weaving the oxen and wagon amidst the debris. Soon he was gone. There was silence. Naran slowly turned her eyes skyward. The Night Shade was coming now. She could feel it. It could come in the day. She knew. The other couldn't. It was still young. Not as experienced as the old one. The ancient one. The one that was coming for Naran.

* * *

Early morning and Fakoud was far down the road. Silomme was left behind. And the ancient stone ruins. The desert nomad had a feeling. Time was short. Short for him. Short for Zothique. A dark cloud was crawling across the barren landscape bringing final absolute death with it. Best to go home to die, Fakoud had decided. So he turned his dromedary south for Zhel.

But memories of recent events plagued him, the nightmare of the fire, and those two women, the young one who had taunted him in the nightmare and the one with the long black hair who had made... Had she? He had awakened naked from the nightmare. She had been there during the night. He remembered her so clearly. She hadn't been something created in his mind like the young woman in the nightmare. The woman with the long black hair had been real.

Fakoud pulled up on the reins. The dromedary stopped. He sat there, his eyes blank, staring. He subconsciously rubbed at the side of his neck. His heart was pulling him back the way he had come. Back toward Silomme. Back toward the ancient stone ruins. His thoughts were on the black haired woman. Lust decided the issue. With a smile, Fakoud turned the dromedary around. At a brisk cantor, he headed back toward the stone ruins.

* * *

Naran had played too long in the streets of abandoned Silomme. Now dusk had settled. Naran knew her mistake. She was well too far from the ruined tavern to make it back before nightfall. But she had to try. She hurried along through gathering shadows. A chill ran up her spine. A Night Shade was nearby. Near enough to be watching her. She quickened her pace. Began to run. She ran down the dusty street and turned into the first alley she came to. It was a narrow alley. The crumbling walls closed in on her.

Then a flutter of wings overhead; the Night Shade had descended from the sky and settled on the edge of a nearby roof. Naran stopped and looked up, saw the Night Shade looking down at her. It was always the same one that taunted Naran, toyed with her like she was a plaything. But this time there was something different. The Night Shade with white skin and long black hair, dressed in a shimmering blue gown, cackled. Her eyes glowed softly in the gathering shadows. Naran's hand went unconsciously to her throat as Lilith leaned forward.

A long forked tongue licked the extended fangs hanging from the roof of Lilith's open mouth. This night was a night to feed. In a motion quicker than Naran's eyes, Lilith arced off the edge of the roof and descended to the alley. Naran turned to run, but wasn't quick enough. Out of the corner of her eyes she saw a whirl of cascading black hair then found herself caught fast. She tried to scream but had no voice. For a moment Naran caught a glimpse of the softly glowing eyes only inches from her face. Those eyes were set deep into the stunningly beautiful face of a woman framed by cascading long black hair.

Lilith snarled. Then in a searing tear of flesh and blood, she buried her fangs deep into Naran's neck. Slowly, as the moments passed, Naran's world began to turn dark. Her mind clouded; her thoughts dimmed. Drained of blood, Naran's life began to ebb away. Sneering at the nearly dead Naran, Lilith extended razor sharp claws and dug into the side of Naran's neck. Fingers disappeared into flesh. Flesh tore; neck bones snapped. In one quick motion Naran's head was torn from her shoulders and tossed across the alley. Lilith paused, inspected the headless body then dropped it. The body toppled to the ground.

Another dead body near the end of Zothique. Lilith was satisfied. She knew the end was near. She'd be the last. She glanced at the severed head lying across the alley. She could see its eyes staring lifeless into the black night sky. *It was only a matter of time for you,* her thoughts voiced to the dead Naran. *Your fate was written long ago.* Lilith paused, listened, and savored. Her senses took in the crumbling village of Silomme. There was silence, and darkness, and death. She grinned, cackled madly then took to the night sky.

With her departure, Silomme was truly dead.

4

It was nearly dark by the time Fakoud had returned to the ancient stone ruins. Blocking the way in the narrow road was an old buckboard wagon pulled by a pair of oxen. The oxen had pulled free of the yoke. They were grazing a short distance away in the shadows, trying to find what little shrub remained for them in the barren landscape. Fakoud pulled up on the reins of his dromedary. There was a shadow at the front of the wagon. The shadow moved. And then a sound. A snarl. Fakoud dismounted, left the dromedary in the road, and started toward the wagon on foot.

Slowly, one step at a time planted quietly on the ground, the desert nomad rounded the old wagon. On the seat was an old man. The same old man that Fakoud had met on the road the day before. He lay back, head tilted at an impossibly odd angle, vacant eyes staring at the rapidly darkening sky. His throat had been ripped out, his neck broken, his head hanging by shredded skin. Trickling blood pooled on the ground beneath the wagon.

Crouched atop the corpse was a young woman. The same young woman that was in Fakoud's nightmare. The name came to him again. Alea Garanase. She raised her head and grinned. Her mouth and chin were stained crimson, running wet with the old man's blood. And her eyes sparkled with an unholy fire in the near darkness. Her grin widened as she sat up. For the first time, Fakoud saw the long curving fangs. Like a cat moving in slow languid motion, the young vampire climbed down from the wagon, her eyes never leaving the desert nomad.

Fakoud was captivated. The power in her eyes froze him where he stood. His eyes followed the slow fluid motion of her body as she approached. Breath caught in his throat as she pushed her body against his and ran her finger lightly over his cheek. Her fingers trailed down the side of his neck and across his shoulder. She leaned forward. A momentary pause, an alluring whisper in his ear. Then her bare fangs extended, she sunk them into his neck.

There was a faint gust of wind. It lifted Garanase's hair. The young vampire paused feeding on Fakoud and looked up. She sniffed the air. And grew nervous. Again she had disobeyed Lilith. Now the ancient vampire was returning. The wind suddenly picked up. Lightning and thunder erupted all about the ancient stone ruins. Just as the wind began to howl through the ancient ruins, Lilith suddenly appeared as if from no where. Garanase dropped Fakoud and he crumbled to the ground.

In a flurry of motion Lilith rose before Garanase. The lightning seemed to turn angry as it crackled across the night sky. Thunder rumbled across the heavens, shaking the ground beneath. The wind continued to howl through the ancient stone ruins. In a flash of lightning Garanase saw Lilith's transformation from a beautiful stately woman, ancient and wise, to the ravaging beast that destroyed and devoured life. The ancient vampire's blue gown billowed on the wind, snapping like a sail; her hair writhed like great black snakes. A fire in her eyes blazed red.

Suddenly Lilith was upon Garanase. It would be a swift and final death for the young woman who had disobeyed the master. The ancient vampire thrust fingertips into Garanase beneath her ribcage. Her hands sliced knife-like into Garanase's chest cavity, found her beating heart, and ripped it from her body. Garanase was astonished. Lilith held the still beating heart up for the young vampire to see as her eyes began to fade. Slipping into final death, Garanase collapsed at Lilith's feet and erupted in consuming fire. The ancient vampire howled with laughter as the heart slowed and finally stopped.

The wind began to diminish. The lightning and thunder faded in the distance. Lilith crushed Garanase's heart between her fingers and then tossed it aside. She turned and looked down at the crumpled form of Fakoud. He lay nearby on the road, his body slowly twitching as he moaned softly. His breathing was shallow, erratic, and growing shallower.

"Ya always did put on a good show; I'll give ya that."

The voice chuckled. It was the voice of an old man. His sudden unexpected appearance had caught Lilith by surprise. She spun on her heels, her eyes wide with anger. She was ready to pounce, but stopped when she saw the old man seated on the bench seat of the wagon next to the dead man. On his lap he held an ancient tome.

"Scye," Lilith said, her voice barely audible.

"'Bout time I close the book, darlin'." Scye was smiling, but his words came from behind Lilith.

She turned, glancing over her shoulder. He stood there in the road, smiling back, gone from the wagon.

Scye nodded to Fakoud. "Best ya kill 'im. Ya can't let 'im live, ya know."

A shadow blacker than night suddenly swam across the ancient stone ruins. It came with a cold wind. The old man looked up and smiled. Lilith crouched in fear. She hadn't feared anything in a long time. But this she did. She knew this shadow and the cold wind that came with it.

"Not yet, ole buddy!" Scye laughed cheerfully. "Ain't time for Zothique's final swan song just yet."

The shadow vanished as suddenly as it had come. And from the dark stepped a man. A young man, a man that Lilith at one time wouldn't hesitate to make her own. But not this time. Not this man. Vilo Sinjar, one time guardian of the gate at the House of Tuluroch. He stopped and watched as Scye turned his attention back to Lilith.

"Ya got 'lotta spunk, I'll say that for ya." Scye chuckled. He grunted as he shifted the ancient tome from one arm to the other then patted the cover. "Ain't many left now," he continued with a smile. "Less 'an you can count on a hand." He lifted his free hand and wiggled his fingers.

Scye took a step forward. Lilith hissed and cautiously stepped back, her eyes darting between Scye and the newcomer Sinjar.

"Now now, darlin'; ain't no need to fear us," Scye continued, "you just git." He waved the fingers of his free hand to shoo her away. "Go on, run along. Ain't much sand left on the hourglass!"

Lilith backed away, fading into the shadows of night. She took to the sky in a flash of lightning and peel of thunder. From high above Zothique she peered down on a nearly dead continent.

"Quite the dramatist, ain't she?" Scye chuckled softly.

"You've a flair for the dramatic yourself," Sinjar said softly after Lilith had gone. He approached and stood next to the wagon.

Scye chuckled. "I suppose I do," he said, the tone and manner of speech markedly different in the face of Mordiggian's avatar, the two of them now alone.

Sinjar turned, looked up at the bench seat of the wagon. He knew Scye would be there. He was, seated next to the dead man. Scye patted the dead man on the head then opened the Book of Destiny.

"The second to last page is filled," Scye said, a finger tapping the image of a dead man on a wagon. "One page left."

"Zothique's final swan song," Sinjar said.

"Yes," Scye replied. He paused, stared into space, contemplative. Then he added, his voice a soft whisper, "History cannot be changed. Or denied."

The Final Swan Song

1

Strahd Zarok was a man with brooding eyes and a dark past he didn't remember. He was a former thief and adventurer. Now he traveled the land on foot in search of adventure. There was something about this place, this Zothique he wandered. There had been many changes over the years as far back as he could remember and then he could remember no more. Recent days he could not remember at all. How he had come to this land of endless desert. How he had known it had once been called *the land of the long red sun*. These he could not remember and it troubled him.

There were things Zarok did know. He knew he was in the north of Zothique, a place once called Dooza Thom. He knew that the cities, towns, and villages of the great continent had long been abandoned. He knew that few remained alive, perhaps no more than could be counted on one hand. He knew that something dark tugged at him from far beyond the mists of his memory, from another place and time. Perhaps it had something to do with the dreams of the hourglass he had been having of late. Perhaps.

He knew he had to keep moving. To somewhere. He shook his head and sighed. Where to go. It was haunting, this perpetual desert. Strange, yet serene. There were no people, no animals, no creatures of any kind. Silence but for the occasional sighing wind. A deathly silence that weighed heavily on Zarok's mind while he wandered in the land of the long red sun. But if there was one thing Zarok had learned in his travels, it was that when things change, it usually wasn't for the better, regardless of how it may have appeared on the surface. Here in the desert it didn't appear as if things were going to change anytime soon.

So Zarok walked on. The bloated red sun began to slip toward the western horizon. The dunes would soon cast long shadows. The night would come. It would be a cold night here in the north of Zothique. Here in a land once called Dooza Thom. Again he would have to rest in the cold desert night with sand all around and the ancient fading stars above. But then he saw the mirage, or at least he figured it to be a mirage.

A mirage was not an uncommon occurrence when one has been walking through a desert for the greater part of time immeasurable. Yet, if it were a mirage, it was the most realistic mirage Zarok had ever encountered. It was water. Massive amounts of water. This was not some little dainty oasis with a couple of bent palm trees erupting from the sand. This was an ocean. Well, perhaps a sea, but a very large sea. Zarok had prayed to the gods of... for water, but he hadn't counted on this.

It was like being on the coast of Ustaim again. Or the coast of Calyz. Those were faded memories. No matter. Zarok ran and ran and ran and got no closer. Then it was gone. Faded into nothing. Just the sand remained. As far as the eye could see. Sand. It was a letdown and Zarok sighed his disappointment. *By the cold wind of Morddigian,* he grumbled a curse in his thoughts. Somewhere in the vast expanse of desert that covered Zothique, Mordiggian heard that course and smiled.

The heat of the day and trudging through endless sand had tired Zarok. He peered about, found himself at the base of a great dune. As good a place as any for some rest. So he curled up on the sand and closed his eyes. A soft whisper of wind across his ears lulled him to sleep. He dreamed the dream again. The enormous hourglass, strangely rotating about an axis tilted at a forty five degree angle, the sand slowly running to the bottom. Time was running out.

Zarok awoke and struggled to his feet. His thoughts were on the dream. The tilted hourglass and something new. There had been a name. Maleva.

* * *

Three demons passed through heavy black clouds. Below them was a churning sea. Cold and stormy, the sea pitched the little boat with passenger between wave crests. It was a young world, dark and violent except for the small oasis. The Garden. And the passenger in the small boat had fled that oasis. The task of the demons was to bring her back.

Thunder vaulted across the heavens. Lightning crackled and hissed, streaking between clouds and sea. The demons dropped out of the cloud cover and hovered for a moment amidst the violence of the storm. Their black cloaks and long white hair rode the howling wind. In the dull light their white skin appeared ashen gray. The white light of their eyes shown brilliant in the gloom as they peered at the small boat on the surface of the churning sea below. Senoy, Sansenoy, and Semangelof descended to hover just above the small boat and its passenger.

The young woman in the boat turned her eyes to the stormy sky. She was naked, her skin and long black hair soaked by the torrent of rain. In the darkness she could see the three pairs of brilliantly shining points of light. In a flash of lightning she could see the forms of the demons, their cloaks and long hair fluttering on the wind, their ashen faces staring down at her.

"Why have you come?" she pleaded. "What do you want of me?"

When the demons spoke, their lips didn't move. Still, the young woman heard their words in her thoughts.

You must return to the Garden. All will be as before, came the voice of Senoy.

"No! no!" the young woman cried out. "I will be second to no one! I will walk behind no one!"

We shall drown you in the sea, said the voice of Sansenoy.

"Leave me!" the young woman cried. "I was created only to cause sickness!" Her eyes narrowed and her voice turned angry and dark as she pointed at the three demons. "I swear to God..."

A sickness it shall be, interrupted the voice of Sansenoy. *You shall seduce men and cause harm to mothers and pregnant women.*

You shall kill all that's living and green, and you shall drink the blood of the living, the voice of Senoy added.

You shall cause disease and death, continued the voice of Semangelof, *and for this, each day one hundred of your kind shall die. So it shall be until the end of time.*

Time shall know you as Lilitu, Lamashtu, Norea, Naamah, Strix, Bathory, began Senoy.

The Shadow, the Seductress, the Screech Owl, the Seven Witches of Sumer, the Whore of Babylon, continued Semangelof.

Lilith the First and Lilith the Last, said the voice of Sansenoy. *You shall live a living death unto the end of time.*

In a flash of lightning, the young woman saw one of the demons slowly begin to raise a hand; a long white finger pointed toward her. *Remember this day,* came the voice of Senoy. *It shall be a day you shall come to regret.*

Then in another flash of lightning, the demons were gone.

The young woman stared into the stormy heavens and saw...

...the stars of a distant future. The stars had faded, were dying even as the world was dying. Even as Zothique was dying. The ancient vampire shook her head. The sudden memory of so long ago startled Lilith. She had never before turned her thoughts back to the beginning, to her beginning. It was as though the memory had been forced upon her. Chilled, she stared wearily into the black night to where the sand and sky met on the distant unseen horizon. Then she felt the presence again. That same malevolent dark presence that had been shadowing her. It was out there. Watching and waiting.

2

The night had passed. It had been quiet, uneventful. Cold. Now Zarok was up and moving again. In the sky was the same bloated red sun. Under foot, the same endless desert. Trudging through the sand was a difficult task. But this morning, it was the last thing on Zarok's mind. Simply put he didn't care. He was preoccupied with his recurring dream. It had started simple enough – a brief glimpse of pouring sand. But each time he dreamed, there was something different. The pouring sand gave way to an hourglass. Then a larger hourglass. Thcn a tiltcd hourglass. Thcn thc name – Maleva. It had caused a faint remembrance of some other place. Some other time.

Zarok stopped; the name kept popping up in his thoughts. "Maleva," he voiced the thought softly.

A vague remembrance, but nothing more. He wandered on, lost in timeless timelessness, not knowing how far he had gone or even in which direction. It really didn't matter. The hourglass in his mind tilted, further upright, the sand running faster, leading to the end... *The end of what?* He grinned and then laughed aloud. His laughter reverberated across the vast desert of the land of the long red sun. *The sun, the sand – I must be going mad!* The laughter began to dwindle to a chuckle. And then he stopped.

Images formed in Zarok's mind. They were images of the past, events he'd lived, people he'd met. Come and gone. Now was only – now. And *now* was what was important. Zarok no longer had any use for the past. There was nothing there but shaded memories. Some good. Some bad. Some not remembered. He shrugged. Just illusions, shades burned away by the bloated disk in the sky of the land of the long red sun.

It was a meaningless past that didn't matter. Zarok brushed the thoughts away as he trudged up the side of a large sand dune and stopped at its crest. His eyes went wide. Before him beyond the dune was a small oasis with a small dwindling pool, a few clusters if green brush, and two towering palm trees. Zarok licked his lips. His thoughts turned to the alkali content of the water, but his thirst outweighed his concern. He stumbled down the dune and to the pool's edge, nearly falling into the water as he dropped to his knees. He bent over, stuck his face into the water, his long hair soaking up the surprisingly cool refreshing and untainted liquid.

Zarok drank until it hurt then rolled over on his back and stared into the orange sky. His hair trailed into the pool, his shirt collar soaking up water cool on his neck. He smiled a smile of content, his thoughts of the past dispelled, his mind on the here and now. And then the sound came to his ears. He caught his breath and listened. Faint sounds, but near. Very near. And it sounded like...*bells*?

The bloated red sun caught Zarok's eyes as he sat up and turned in the direction of the sound. He squinted. There was a figure in the glare of the sun, silhouetted against the glow. It was the silhouette of a woman in a long dress, a woman with long hair. The woman was moving toward Zarok, and he heard the soft tinkling of bells as she walked. She crossed the angle of the sun so that Zarok could see her face for the first time. She smiled as she approached then stood before him. There was a moment of silence. Her smile widened.

"Strahd Zaroskaya," she said softly, music in her voice. "It's been a long time."

"Who are you?" Zarok questioned.

"Does it matter?"

"Yes, it matters!" Zarok replied, indignant.

The woman laughed. "Alright," she said, "I'm the first and the last. You once knew me as Magda. A long long time ago."

"Magda," Zarok said the name.

The woman nodded. "Yes, Magda."

Zarok glanced at the jewels in Magda's hair and the ankle bells she wore. Again there was a faint memory of a far away place. Another time. He closed his eyes and listened to his thoughts, trying to remember. But the memory faded and there was only the wind.

*　*　*

How dare he, the Wicked Priest of Judea, know not the coming of the Apocalypse. He shall be destroyed as with all those wicked. As with the Seductress from the beginning who shall die at the end of time. And the end of time is near...

Matthatias sat back from his parchment. He had been working since early morning, transcribing in his native Hebrew the warnings against the Seductress. His mind wandered as he wrote the lines. Even here in the small hermit community of In Ir ha-Melah, the City of Salt, the lure and temptation of her did not go unfelt.

There was no time to waste. The end was near. The scrolls had to be completed and stored in the caves above In Ir ha-Melah. Agents of the Angel of Darkness were coming and great forces marshaled against the righteous. Matthatias smiled. He knew they would be met and defeated. The Seductress would be defeated. Sadness suddenly overcame Matthatias as he continued the transcription.

'Woe and disaster to all who possess her!
  'And desolation to all who hold her!
'For her ways are the ways of death,
  'and her paths are the roads of sin,
  'and her tracks are pathways to iniquity,
  'and her by-ways are rebellious wrong-doings.
'Her gates are gates of death,
  'and from the entrance of the house
  'she sets out towards Sheol.
'None of those who enter there will ever return,
  'and all who possess her will descend to the Pit
'She lies in wait in secret places,...'

A shadow suddenly crossed the table in the transcription room where Matthatias sat. He looked up. A wraith-like figure stood in the doorway. She was lithe, wore a flowing gown, and long black hair fell over her shoulders. She smiled and motioned for Matthatias to follow. He did.

3

Somewhere on a sand covered wind swept plateau they stood in a circle, facing the center. They stood on a flat rock formation that jutted from the sand like the roof of a mastaba in a far away place, long long ago. A place long vanished to time. Their number was eight, all clad in black hooded robes, even the small grotesque figure that rocked side to side, teetering on the toes of this form his avatar had taken.

Avatars. For they were not men. They were gods. The last of the gods that presided over the dying continent of Zothique. They had come from the earth, the sea, from lands once called Ilcar and Yoros, from the aether between the nether regions. They had come for this one last gathering, a summons at the behest of the maiden goddess Ohjal. Their words were not spoken words carried on the howling wind. Their words echoed in their thoughts.

You've interest in this common thief, Zarok? Vergama said.

The maiden goddess Ohjal replied in their thoughts. *Zarok is Zaroskaya. I wish to return him from whence he came. To his people and rightful place in time. His place is with them. Not here to die as this land dies.*

The soft maniacal chuckling of Yuckla, the small grotesque god of laughter, echoed in their thoughts as heads turned, Morddigian to Basatan to Geol to Ililot to Thasaidon, while absent eyes peered deep from the hood of Vergama to Ohjal across the circle. She stared.

Their came a short curt laugh from Vergama and then the words: *He would die as all the others.*

The last page of your book isn't written. There is still time.

Only three remain, Vergama replied.

Three? Ojhal was puzzled.

Three, Vergama said without explanation.

You still have Lilith. She had worn many faces. She is the last as she claimed she'd be.

Her fate is already decided, yet not written. An armless sleeve rose and pointed across the circle to Ojhal as Vergama's voice again echoed in their thoughts. *Go to Zaroskaya and return him from whence he came. Tell Lilith that her fate shall soon come to her.*

Where once stood a figure cloaked in a black robe, there now stood an old Gypsy woman dressed in a long ankle length dress with embroidered patterns, flowered blouse, blue apron, and red bandanna atop her head. A large golden ring hung from her left ear and a necklace of coins was draped around her neck.

Behind her waited a small horse cart pulled by a single horse, an oil lantern suspended from a curved wooden stave. She turned to the horse cart, climbed onto the bench seat, and slowly road away. Gypsy bells rang across the desert, soft but audible above the howling wind. The old Gypsy woman suddenly pulled up on the reins and looked back. The seven remaining gods were gone. Only the howling wind and swirling sand remained.

* * *

There was a sound, a soft tinkling of bells, but not Magda's bells. Zarok turned and looked. In the distance out on the desert sands was a Gypsy horse cart drawn by a single horse. The horse cart was approaching the oasis. He and Magda waited. The horse cart pulled to a stop. There was an old Gypsy woman seated on the horse cart's bench seat. A lantern swung gently on a wooden stave affixed to the side of the cart. There was silence as the old woman stared at them. Zarok stared back, inquisitive, wondering. Magda, her head lowered, stared through narrowed eyes that glared hatred. She knew this old Gypsy woman from the past. It was she who had spirited Zaroskaya to safety long long ago from a place called Vasaria. Though Magda recognized the old Gypsy woman, she failed to recognize the truth, a fact that didn't go unnoticed by Maleva.

"You remember," the old Gypsy said, a smile crossing her face.

"Yes, I know you," Magda replied. "How is it that you are...?"

"It matters not," Maleva said. Her eyes shifted to Zarok. "I've come for him."

Magda laughed. "You took him from me once, long ago; you won't take him again." Her words were soft, tinged with anger. "Do you know who I am?"

There was a brief chuckle then Maleva's eyes narrowed. "I've known you from the beginning of time. You can't run away."

"Hey, hey, hey!" Zarok cut into the confrontation. "What is this? Who are you?"

"The old woman is Maleva," Magda answered scornfully.

"Maleva?" Zarok saidd softly as he stared at the old woman.

"Yes," the old Gypsy said softly.

"I've heard your name in my dreams," Zarok said.

"Well that you should, my son," the old woman voiced softly, her words ringing with a strange foreign accent. "Close your eyes, look into your heart. See from whence you've come."

Zarok closed his eyes and saw shadows of the past. Though hazy, the shadows began to clear. There was a Gypsy camp, a celebration, dancing. That night Bela had died. And Talbot was cursed.

"Bela," Zarok said softly of the memory, his eyes still closed.

Maleva smiled.

Magda sneered.

The vision faded. Zarok opened his eyes and glanced at the old Gypsy woman. There was fire in her eyes, a light of intelligence and wisdom. For a moment, Zarok thought that this woman harbored a secret of her own.

"You remember," the old Gypsy woman said.

"I saw images, heard words. That's all."

"You are Gypsy blood, Zaroskaya," Maleva began, her voice soft and guarded. "You know that we know things others do not."

"Zaroskaya," Zarok said suddenly. His eyes quickly glanced between the two women.

"Because that is who you are," Maleva replied. "It's time that you go home."

Zarok stared at the old Gypsy woman. His thoughts drifted.

"You cannot take him from me...," Magda sneered.

"Tell me not what I can and cannot do," Maleva cut the ancient vampire off. The old Gypsy's words were angered. Her stare cold and icy. "You are cursed." Maleva climbed down from the horse cart and stood face to face with Magda. She passed an open palm over Magda's eyes.

"Sleep," Maleva said softly.

The ancient vampire's eyes closed and she slipped to the sand.

"And dream," Maleva continued. "When you awaken, your fate will come for you." The old Gypsy woman turned and reached out a hand to Zarok. "Come," she said softly.

Together they climbed onto the bench seat. With a shake of the reins, the Gypsy horse cart lumbered off, rolling slowly across the desert, the Gypsy bells softly tinkling in the hot desert air. A short distance away, Maleva pulled up on the reins. The cart stopped. She looked back. The oasis was gone. All that remained was Magda asleep in the sand.

4

The Whore of Babylon skirted alleys and byways, making her way through the slums along the Euphrates waterfront. A pause, a hushed whisper, and a wink would bait and hooked them without fail. Babylon's men could not resist her. Babylon's women did nothing. They were frightened of her. The eye she turned to Babylon's men was not the same eye she turned to Babylon's women.

"Come, come this way," the Whore lured men down the dark and twisted alleys of Babylon's slums. The sun was setting, the city darkening. Suddenly the sounds of city revelry fell silent.

Eerily silent.

The castle servants had gone. So had the workmen who had bricked up the door to Erzsebet's room, trapping her inside. Only a small opening remained in the brick wall to pass through food and drink. Erzsebet peered at the bricks. She snickered then cackled. It was a mad cackle.

How dare they, she scoffed silently. *Do you think that can keep me here? A prisoner in this castle? My own home?*

The cackling turned to riotous laughter. Erzsebet had murdered young girls to keep her youth. At least that's what the witnesses had said at her trial. They had no idea. Not the witnesses, nor the judge. They didn't know that Erzsebet was ancient, long before their time. The first woman. She would live long after Cachtice Castle and Hungary had disappeared into the dusts of time. Erzsebet's laughter continued as she turned to the window and peered into the night sky.

The moon was rising full and bright. The ashen glow fed on the stone ruins, the cemetery where she stood, alone, tombstones askew. There was a mausoleum. She turned and looked and smiled as she read the family name on the lintel above the entrance. The name: Karnstein. A hundred years Lilith had spent with the family, guiding the young Countess. First as her governess then as her guardian. Until it was time to leave. A carriage accident provided an excuse. She had fled, disappearing into the woods.

A shadow had skirted the woods, darting between trees. Magda followed, having quietly slipped out of the Gypsy camp. No one had noticed. It was a festive occasion. There was dancing and music and singing. It was a celebration of life. Bela's life. He had died and now the man Talbot was cursed. Just as Bela had been cursed.

Magda stepped out of the shadows into the light of the moon. "Strahd Zaroskaya," she said softly and smiled.

Zarokskaya turned. "Magda," he said. He paused, glanced at the moon in the night sky then turned his eyes back to Magda. "It's dangerous to be alone in the woods tonight. The moon is full. The wolf will be about."

"I'm not alone," Magda replied. She smiled was she reached up and brushed Zaroskaya's cheek with her fingers. Suddenly there was a noise. Magda paused, listened. It wasn't the wolf. It was bells. Gypsy horse cart bells. Magda turned. There was nothing there but shadows and the softly ringing bells. When she turned back, Zaroskaya was gone. "Strahd?" she questioned...

Then woke to the sighing wind and the Gypsy horse cart bells ringing in her dreams. Lilith caught her breath. She suddenly sat up and peered about. The bloated sun rested hideously on the horizon. The oasis was gone. No pool of water. No swaying palms. No brush. No Zaroskaya and Maleva. Only sand as far as the eye could see and horse cart tracks leading away, over a dune, and beyond. She felt a sudden feeling of intense terror the likes of which Lilith had never before experienced.

Lilith scrambled to her feet. She spun in a circle and stopped. Her eyes befell a figure standing atop a nearby sand dune. It stood motionless; a shadow in the light of the bloated red sun. And it was staring back at her through dark and deep set eyes, pinpoints of light twinkling in the iris's. This was the source of Lilith's sudden fear. This was fate come for her, handiwork of Thasaidon, God of Evil.

Thoughts enraged, Lilith started toward the thing atop the dune. A faint trace of recognition slowed her approach then she stopped as the full weight of recognition fell upon her. This thing was the desert nomad beset upon by Garanase at the ruins outside Silomme, the same desert nomad that Lilith had failed to destroy at the behest of Vergama. Now he lived, but not like Lilith.

Korani Fakoud was not a creature of bloodlust like Lilith. He was neither alive nor dead. What was once the desert nomad had been disassembled and reconstructed by Thasaidon. Although he still had a semblance of humanity, very little of Fakoud that remained was human. The beast stood a good nine feet tall, balanced on clawed feet that resembled a reptile. His arms were triple-jointed and hung nearly to the ground. Hands had been replaced by taloned claws. Skin was tough, thick, and leathery. The skull had been opened, the brain removed and replaced by something that only Thasaidon could know and explain. The god had delighted in his creation. The thing was dark, monstrous, and excelled in inflicting excruciating pain, torment, and terror.

The beast that had been Fakoud raised a clawed hand. In it he held an hourglass. The thing grinned then threw the hourglass to the ground. The timepiece shattered on cobblestone. The desert of north Zothique, the former land of Dooza Thom, was gone. Instead, the beast Fakoud and Lilith stood facing one another in the cobblestoned courtyard of a chateau. They had transcended space and time.

This was the chateau along the road to Silomme, yet another chateau, another Silomme. This chateau hadn't caught fire nor lain in crumbling ruins. It still existed, cold and dark, deserted for centuries between worlds in a nether region where time was not measured. It needn't be. Forever in this black purgatory with no sunrise, a soft yellow light would glow from a second story window, shadows to dance upon walls, Lilith's voice to forever howl pain and torment.

Here in this chateau, the beast Fakoud would invade her mind, tear her mind asunder, render her a bubbling caricature of a woman. Her mind would be forever filled with horrible images while the beast Fakoud would do terrible and unmentionable things to her in the endless black between worlds. And so it would be for eternity.

* * *

There was a legend that a small Gypsy caravan plied the trade routes between the small villages of Vasaria. Late at night a Gypsy dancer with long black hair and ankle bells danced in the fire light. Among those gathered was a man. He wore an earring, a red bandanna. He was called Zaroskaya.

In the firelight of the Gypsy camp Zaroskaya leaned forward and smiled at the dancer, La Riana, a twinkle in his eye. La Riana smiled back. He hadn't a care in the world, for he was at peace with himself. His memory had been given back to him. And his home.

* * *

Vergama sat on a rock, the Book of Destiny in his lap. The Book was complete. He closed it. The god sighed, chuckled, and nodded contentment to the howling wind. He was satisfied with his handiwork, having guided humanity to the end of its days, to the end of Zothique. Now it was time to go. A land with no people needed no gods. Vergama rose from the rock. He paused, looked at his book, and smiled. Then laying the book atop the rock, he turned and walked away.

The sun was setting on Zothique. The bloated red sun. Blood red. The wind howled endlessly across the desolate landscape. Time passed. Wind and sand forced open the pages of the book. The pages were worn, tattered, ancient. Slowly weathering away. It was all that remained of the world. For now the gods were gone. There was no one left to tell the story. No one left to remember.

The gods had scattered throughout time to take up abodes from which to oversee the destiny of humankind once again. As the bloated red sun set on the windswept continental desert that Zothique had become, the hourglass of the gods again turned. The sands of humanity began to trickle through.

Printed in Great Britain
by Amazon